PASS GUARD AT YPRES

PASS GUARD
AT YPRES

by

Ronald Gurner

CASEMATE
uk
Oxford & Philadelphia

Published in Great Britain and
the United States of America in 2016 by
CASEMATE PUBLISHERS
10 Hythe Bridge Street, Oxford OX1 2EW, UK
and
1950 Lawrence Road, Havertown, PA 19083, USA

Paperback Edition: ISBN 978-1-61200-411-2
Digital Edition: ISBN 978-1-61200-412-9 (epub)

A CIP record for this book is available from the British Library

Printed in the Czech Republic by FINIDR

For a complete list of Casemate titles, please contact:

CASEMATE PUBLISHERS (UK)
Telephone (01865) 241249
Fax (01865) 794449
Email: casemate-uk@casematepublishers.co.uk
www.casematepublishers.co.uk

CASEMATE PUBLISHERS (US)
Telephone (610) 853-9131
Fax (610) 853-9146
Email: casemate@casematepublishing.com
www.casematepublishing.com

TO ALL WHO SERVED AT YPRES

"WE BAND OF BROTHERS"

TO YOUTH

Why should you, living in a world now free,
 Read of dead evil things of long ago?
   If men fought thus, why, what is it to you?
   If from the distance hands are stretched, and low
     Faint cries of those that fell and those that slew
   Find utterance, because they haunt me so,
     Telling of agonies you never knew—
What, then, of that? Yet, of your charity,
I ask you, bear you with me, for to me
   Ypres rises mystic in the sunset glow,
   The Menin Road winds where the waters flow,
   And those strange ghosts that ever come and go
   Speak to me sometimes, when the waves beat slow,
Their voices mingled with a Sussex sea.

PAGHAM, 1929.

7

CHAPTER I

I<small>T</small> looked a bit rough, thought Freddy Mann, as he lit another cigarette and absent-mindedly fingered the identity disk which hung about his neck. The sea was getting up, and the wind was freshening. What would it be like to be at sea if it was rough? He had never been to sea before, and he was rather afraid that he might be sick. He would rather not be sick in front of his men; he didn't suppose really that it mattered much, but, as Harry and others at Aldershot had often told him, it was sometimes little things that just made the difference in the men's respect. He didn't think though, on the whole, that he had much to fear on that score. He looked at his platoon, some reclining, packs off, at the side of the quay, some, like Sergeant Mitchell, walking idly up and down. Jolly good platoon, his platoon. He'd had them from the first, and after five months' training he knew them pretty well. Raw enough they'd all been when they first found themselves together in the huts at Witley—himself straight up from his father's little shop at Edenhurst, and the men drafted post-haste from London into the newly formed division, still with civvy hats, boots and great-coats, fit prey for the few Regular N.C.O.s, sergeant-majors and others, to whom had been entrusted, under Colonel Townroe and a handful of "pukka" officers, the task of licking them into shape. Little enough they could do then; there wasn't a better platoon in "K.1" now. They'd had some times together, by Jove! Incidents came into his mind as he sat, a little apart, looking sometimes at them, sometimes at other broken lines of khaki stretching along the quay, and from time to time at the transport in the distance, which they would board at six o'clock. That strange review of January, that winter's morning when their battalion had marched out from Witley, not too well protected against the driving snow, to assemble with other columns which poured across hills and along muddy roads, and wait half-numbed until a car appeared, drove without stopping through the centre of the divisions and left them to disperse; that other review when, as they marched past, Kitchener had stood at the salute, and they had seen in the flesh the leader whose name was already almost legendary; the move in March, when they had marched as a battalion for the first time, fully equipped, from Witley into Aldershot; the three days' training scheme in the early days of spring, when the men had barns for billets, grumbled about their rations, and thought it fun; route marches, field-cooking practice upon the slope by Frensham Pond, field days that grew in scope and intensity as March gave place to April, night operations, musketry courses at Ash Ranges, and day by day the steady routine of Badajos Barracks—he and his platoon had had time through this to know each other well enough. He'd miss this life, he rather thought. Better this than the dull round in his father's little shop at Edenhurst; better, too, the companionship of Harry, "Robbie," Toler, Bill and "Sammy" in the company mess than the little country circle in which his father, mother and sisters moved. He'd miss the weekly show at the Hippodrome, and the return to the little quartermaster's house at Badajos and drinks at midnight, the teas at Buzzacott's, the fortnightly leave to Town, where, with the dashing Mare or Copeland, he had packed very considerably more into the few hours at his disposal before rejoining the crowded 10.50 at Waterloo than during any previous stay of long or short duration at his aunt's at Peckham. Five months of it—but perhaps, after all, those five months were long enough; they were impatient now, officers and men, in the company, the battalion, and the whole division; they wanted to get there. They got more and more irritated when some grizzled old cynic like Kennedy, "A" Company Commander, growled that they'd have plenty of it before they'd finished. They talked interminably about the news from the Front, Neuve Chapelle, the gas attack on Ypres. As delay followed delay and the company had been keyed up for departure only for rumours to prove false once more, they wondered whether they were to be kept there in Aldershot for three years or the duration; and then, just when impatience was turning to resentment, there had come quite suddenly the renewed excitement in the orderly room, the meticulous inspections of kit and barracks, the hectic visits to Field Stores, the three days' final leave, the march through a starry night in May from Badajos to Farnborough—training was over and they were for it now, and they were glad. It wasn't, indeed, exactly the sort of way in which it was to be expected that soldiers should sally forth to war: there should have been a march with bands playing and colours flying, through streets thronged with cheering crowds, and embraces and fond farewells at stations hung with flags. But many things, as Freddy Mann knew already, in this war were strange: he rather thought that previously a company hadn't been drawn up just before entrainment, and a black-looking object composed of gauze and cotton wool carefully issued to every officer and man, with instructions for its use quietly given out by a level-voiced Colonel in the R.A.M.C., who finished by remarking in the same even, passionless tones in which he had already spoken that "loss of this respirator, or even a few minutes' delay in its adjustment, may result in instant death." That was new to all, but to him other things were new as well: this sea crossing, for example. They would soon be there now—just this few hours' wait at Southampton, then the night voyage across. Well, he was ready for it, but what would it all be like? He looked at his respirator, and fingered the handle of his pistol. What sort of a crossing would it be—and what would it be like on the other side?

CHAPTER II

MADAME FOUQUIÈRE sat in the sunshine outside the main estaminet at Watten, and beamed as she looked on her domain. Her smile, like her figure, was expansive; well it might be, for the greater part of what she surveyed was directly or indirectly hers. The old man, working at the manure heap across the road, battered straw hat upon his head, was her father; the children just in front of her were her younger son's and daughter's offspring; the estaminet itself was hers, as were the little houses that lined the lane to the left of where she sat, the barns and sheds directly opposite, the geese and chickens that wandered in the garden plot and upon the highway, the dog that basked beside her, the cows that chewed the cud lazily in the field beyond the line of poplar trees, the yoked dog-team which was drawing a small heavily laden cart home along the *pavé*, the fields round the cross roads in the middle distance, and the farm upon the hillside, now made over to her son-in-law, where her daughter lived. Without question, next to the Mayor, Madame Fouquière was the lady of chief estate in Watten, and as for the Mayor himself—"La, la," Madame Fouquière would say, "he is rich now, for the English pay him well for billets, but in himself that Beaugard is of little import, and his farm is small; but as for me—*quant moi*—what if my man is dead? Mayor he may be, that Beaugard, but *enfin*, what would you have, Beaugard or Fouquière?" Few in Watten or elsewhere were to be found to dispute her claim, and the reign of Madame Fouquière was peaceful. This was as it should be, for peace abode in Watten. For fifty years Madame Fouquière had known the little commune, and it was now in all essentials as it had been in those early days when traces of the invader were beginning to disappear, and northern agricultural France awoke to find herself free and turned herself to her work and her content again. Even now, after nine months of war, the peace of Watten was almost undisturbed, and there was but little change. The men had gone, indeed— Jacques, Madame's son-in-law, her nephews Pierre and Rupert, and many others, leaving but those such as her lazy old father, *ce vieux ça, Père* Hamblin, and the women to guard the farms and tend the crops. Always now there was that mutter on the horizon to the east, sometimes swelling to a sudden roar, and at night the dancing lights and flashes in the heavens; and the soldiers passed through week by week, French at first, her own countrymen, with their blue and red uniforms, who waved so cheerily and kissed so gallantly and paid so very little; then British, or perhaps Canadian, but all alike to her, clad in that strange khaki, marching always so neatly, leaving her barns and estaminet always so clean, paying always so much, happy there in Watten, yet always, it seemed, wishing so to take the road towards the east. These things indeed were new, but the rest remained; the Forêt d'Eperlecques, stretching

its green and shady length to greet the midday heat along
the hills, the stream eddying lazily between the banks and
the moss-covered arches of the little bridge at the bottom
of the road, Watten itself, the home of her and hers for
generations, which *le bon Dieu*, not forgetting those
flowers and lighted candles which stood ever before his
Mother's image in church and on the wayside shrine, had
so far spared. Ah well, if prayers and candles could avail,
with Jacques and her men away and les salles Boches
just beyond those hills, there was need indeed for both.
He would spare them still, and grant to those away a safe
return. In the meantime one takes things as they come:
her daughters will work and her grandsons, *les gamins*,
and Yvonne, until the time shall come for her to bear her
Jacques his child, and *ce vieux* her father, he above all shall
work, for all his laziness, but it is not for her to till the fields,
or tend the cattle, while there are these others round: for
her the estaminet, the letting of the barns, the watching
of that baggage in the kitchen and of Beaugard, rogue of
rogues, who would keep her money as he does the money
of those others, were she not there week by week outside
the door when the officer came to pay. And for the rest, on
these afternoons of early summer, when others were about
their business—as it was well that they should be, and she
would see to it that they were—the chair before the door,
and the knitting, and the talk to the officer who happened,
as one so often happened, to be sitting by her side; as this
officer, for example, this quiet one, who with the others
had lived for a week in her estaminet, and who would go,

he thought, tomorrow. "*Bébé*" she had named him from the first, and she called him now *mon Bébé* openly, a name which suited him and which he did not seem to mind. They had been very young, some of the officers who had stayed with her as they passed through Watten, and these who had now come, who called themselves "K.1" and knew nothing of war, were for the most part younger still, but even of them he was the youngest. Why, did he even shave? she wondered, for he was almost like a girl to look at, not tall, not broad or strong, and his cheeks and face still pink and white, though browner now than when he came. Here he was as usual, the day's route march over, polishing the leather belt which his servant had already made so clean, smoking what these English called a fag, listening from time to time to the sound of the guns which she knew well, but which was still strange to him, wondering whether they were nearer or farther away and whether they were ours or theirs. How they were funny, these English soldiers, who had come, it seemed, almost from the nursery to the war; but they marched well, and their men obeyed them, and, like those others who had passed before, they wanted to go forward to the east; which Madame was glad to see, for already some had passed, coming into Watten by the other road, who had not wanted to return, and had told her things about the trenches which as yet these officers, even the great dark Harree, could scarcely know. *Bébé*, like the others, wanted to be up and gone; he had just said so: he would not sit there, quiet, telling her about his home and England, and his friend, one Muriel, after that afternoon.

16

"Although we shall be sorry to go," he continued, "I shall, anyway. We didn't expect anything of this when we landed last week at——" He stopped. He would not say where they had landed, although she knew quite well. "They told us we should go straight up——"

"To Ypres."

Freddy Mann turned round with an almost startled expression to Madame.

"How do you know? I haven't told you."

"Know? It is easy, that, to know, *mon petit*. It is always Ypres. Sometimes La Bassée or Armentières for a time, but always *enfin* Ypres. I see them when they go, and just sometimes when they return. You go to Ypres, *parbleu*. It is the lot of all."

"Well, I don't know that we mind if we do," as Freddy Mann lit another cigarette. "Interesting sort of place to see; we've heard a lot about it. But it's all the same to us, you know. They said when we got to——"

"Havre."

"Know that, too, do you? Well, anyway, they said then we might be sent to Gallipoli. Glad we've come to France, though. It's the Boche our crowd joined up to fight. Besides——" He looked round. "Places like this are worth coming to. Wonder if there are many of them."

"It is France, *mon Bébé*; yes."

"You ought to have heard Sammy in the Forest this morning. You know Sammy, don't you—that rather tubby chap—fellow that sings, you know. Sings and eats a lot."

"Yes."

17

"Well, he fairly let himself go when we had the midday easy. Started spouting poetry and singing like Caruso, till Harry choked him off. Just like Sammy; it doesn't take much to work him up. But it certainly was tophole, you know. The birds singing, and the sunlight coming through the leaves, and the white road and everything so peaceful. Think the men noticed it, too, as well as us."

He put down his Sam Browne for a few moments in silence, looking down the lane that led away from the high road opposite them.

"Seem almost to have bought this place, you know. The battalion's all over it. We've named bits of it among ourselves. That's Harry's Corner, and there's Toler's Copse, and there where Sammy's platoon is, that's the Zoo. You'll miss us when we've gone."

"Others will follow. There are always more coming up; they say there is no end to you, the British."

"Suppose not—we're just beginning to come now. About time. Devil of a time the war's gone on already. Can't last much longer. But I'm glad it's lasted as long as this. Gives a fellow a chance to get out and see a bit of life, you know. We've got across, anyway. Bet half the people in England will never get as far as that. But all our crowd joined up early, that's why we've got out soon. And it's Ypres you think we're going to?"

Madame nodded.

"Ah, well." Freddy Mann suddenly got up and straightened his tunic. "P'raps you're right. And good luck to it; I shan't mind if it is. Must be off now—time for rations, and then I've got the post to do. Ypres—don't suppose it'll be quite as peaceful there, I must say. Sammy'll have to find another tune. Funny if you're wrong, Madame, and we don't go there at all. I'll let you know—oh, no, I can't— forgot that, otherwise I would. Can't tell, you know, you may be wrong."

"It is always Ypres, *mon Bébé*. I have seen it from the beginning—it is always so. First our *poilus*, then the British, the Canadians, then you again, the British: by different roads perhaps, Steenvoorde, Hazebrouck, La Bassée or Armentières—but always at the end is Ypres."

CHAPTER III

"IT looks to me," said Derek Robinson, as he blew reflectively into the bowl of his pipe, "it looks to me as if we were nearly there."

"Aye!" Jack Wilson had joined the forces after a short but not uneventful career in a windjammer, and his conversation savoured of the nautical. "We'll make Ypres soon: get off my mapcase, you swine," as he dumped Freddy Mann bodily two feet farther away from where he had previously sat. "What's the news, Skipper?"

Captain Toler, fresh from the temporary Battalion Headquarters, approached the group sitting by the roadside outside Vlamertinghe with something more than his usual importance of manner. His step was more determined, the lines between his eyebrows more deeply graven, the tug at his bushy black moustache even more vicious than was generally the case.

"Gawd, we're for it," as the irreverent Malcolm leaned back against his pack and munched another bar of chocolate. "Hold hard all. Well, Skipper, who's won the war?"

"Now look, Captain Harry, look, gentlemen." Captain Toler rapidly approached with one finger firmly planted on a certain point on his talc-faced mapcase. He looked quickly round. "Mr. Wilson, perhaps you had better rejoin your company; Captain Massy Vane will need you—and this is no time for merriment."

"Right-ho: six bells it is: avast ahoy. Lewis, don't forget the milk. Cheerio all," and Jack's stubby form rolled down the road towards his recumbent platoon.

"Now, gentlemen," as Captain Toler, now safe with his own circle, looked from his second in command to his subalterns in turn. "Now look, Robbie—Mr. Robinson— look, Mr. Mann; are you attending, Mr. Shepherd?"

Sammy Shepherd's attention was for the moment diverted, as it was so often to be diverted in the near future, by the sudden screech of a shell, the identification and classification of which as friendly or hostile appeared to be of paramount importance.

"Yes, Skipper, yes, I see—yes."

"Well, then, now"—having fixed the roving eyes of Shepherd—"perhaps we'd better have the Sergeant-Major—ah there you are, Sergeant-Major. Well, we're to move at once to the Ramparts and join the 1st Battalion in the line tonight. Have you got Ypres on the map, Mr. Malcolm—square K2. Have you got your map, Mr. Mann? Always have your map on active service. Have you got Vlamertinghe? Good."

A cloud of smoke obscured for a moment the pointing finger as the Skipper puffed vigorously at his pipe.

"Well, then, we move by the Poperinghe-Ypres Road, past the Goldfish Château, to the Ramparts, then on to the line—we move as a battalion to the Ramparts, Captain

Harry, and by companies with guides to the line—and there we find the 1st Battalion. We shall be attached to them for training purposes probably for a week, but it's not quite certain yet how long. It's 2.30 now; we move at 4. Now remember, gentlemen, remember, Robbie lad, remember, Mr. Mann, all I've told you—we're going into the thick of it now. Remember, on the march, march discipline first, last and all the time. And remember, when we get to the line, always take bearings, use prismatic compasses—keep in line with flanks or platoons in front—no smoking, dead silence, and if things happen remember that the men will look to you."

•   •   •   •   •

The afternoon wore on, punctuated by occasional further exhortations and sundry inspections of company transport and kit by the over-conscientious Skipper. Freddy Mann knew already by heart all that his O.C. had or could possibly have to say, and there were other matters here to engage his attention. To the traffic he was to a certain extent already accustomed. Those lines of men moving east and west, those guns and limbers, ambulances and occasional cars had passed him on the road by which they had travelled during the last three days from peaceful Watten through Steenvoorde, St. Sylvestre Capel, Abeele, St. Jan ter Biezen and Poperinghe. But today there were other things to see as well. That howitzer by the line of willows, for example, fixing in a leisurely but purposeful fashion a shell every fifteen minutes; the Anti-aircraft Battery, which Freddy Mann had already learned to call an Archie, standing in retreat just up the lane; the three sausages on the road between them and Ypres; the ambulance which he'd just passed along the road with a load of bandaged men; the comings and goings round the C.C.S. in the farmhouse a few hundred yards away. Nobody, thought Freddy Mann, seemed in any hurry; nobody, save perhaps their own raw selves, showed any particular sign of emotion; it was a fine afternoon, and war seemed a leisurely business on the road to Ypres. Perhaps in Ypres itself it would be rather different. He was sorry that he could not see Ypres. It lay there down the road in the middle distance beyond the caissons, with the smoke drifting over it. He wanted to get there to see it, now that he had got so near as this, and he was glad when at 4.30 the battalion collected itself, shook itself together and took the road past the R.E. dump, the advanced corps battery positions, the Goldfish Château, the Divisional H.Q. and on to the Asylum.

Ypres was plain enough now before them, and around them the country grew more desolate and sinister. The road led past a ruined farm-house here, a row of torn pollards there; shell holes, some recent, because more frequent. The men they saw were moving not in mass but in single lines or scattered groups. A curious dead smell was perceptible in the evening air. The road was straight now, straight ahead to Ypres. Freddy Mann trudged on, following Robbie's platoon sergeant, who grumbled on his way a few yards in front of him, passing down occasional orders and watching flickers and stabs of fire in the sky in front of him as the darkness began to fall. Oh well, it was quiet enough, anyway. Here they were, past the Asylum now, and in the narrow street that led over the bridge and past the water-tower on the outskirts of the town. This was Ypres: it seemed to have drawn them from Watten almost as if it were a magnet. It was better than he expected— better except for the sickening stench. That was gas, he supposed, or dead bodies—perhaps a bit of both. That was the prison, was it, on the left; he'd heard of that. And here where the road curved round to the right and to the left again, here was the Cloth Hall and the Square. Pity he couldn't see the Hall a little better, but it was a dark night and he had to keep in touch with Robbie just ahead, and it wasn't the sort of place at which they'd halt, to judge from the accounts he'd already heard. Like slugs, the platoon ahead of him moved on towards the ramparts. That was where the guides were going to meet them. So they'd got there, and now there was nothing to do but to lie down by the side of the broken street and wait. No doubt about it, they were getting near: the crack of rifles and machine guns was incessant—star shells flickered round them, shells came with greater frequency overhead. Where he and Robbie sat there wasn't much to see but a calvary standing in a ruined church and rows of dug-outs in the ramparts on their right, but just over the ramparts there lay the canal and the Menin Road. That was the way the Skipper said they were to go tonight. Good luck to it.

Nothing had gone wrong yet; the men seemed cheerful, the night was fine, a shell had burst near him and he hadn't been afraid and . . .

"Bit of all right this, sir."

Freddy Mann looked round to see standing by him the heavy form of his batman, Private Bamford. He wondered exactly what he intended to convey. The phrase itself is nothing but the King's pawn opening to soldiers' conversation, and the only fitting answer to it, "Not arf it ain't," is one that it is not easy for an officer to use. He nodded and awaited elucidation.

"This ain't arf all right, it seems to me," came the low growl in which Private Bamford usually spoke. "Blimy, sir, 'ere we are within a stone's throw of 'em, as the sayin' goes, and walkin' about large as life, an' nothing happens. Best of this 'ere war, that is—yer knows where yer are, when yer for it and when yer not. In South Africa now—I tell yer yer couldn't walk about like this in South Africa, what with them Boers be'ind each kopje, and arf the in'abitants with shot guns be'ind yer back. Didn't stroll about there, same as if we was at a picnic, I can tell yer. Snowballin' this, I calls it, compared to South Africa. That'll be the Cloth Hall, I take it, that there." He nodded carelessly across his shoulder.

"That's it; we're in the Salient now all right. Glad you think it snowballing. Men seem happy enough so far."

"All right, they are, sir; you leave 'em to me. We knows each other, as the sayin' goes. S'long as old Uncle B. is with 'em—that's me, sir—that's what they call me off parade. Good fellers, though, they are. Stout-'earted. Swears well:

always a good sign that, if a man can get it across with 'is language."

"They?" Freddy Mann hardly liked to voice the question that had been so often in his mind. "You think they'll be all right—when the bullets come? Sometimes I—we—just wonder a bit, you know. It's—hard to tell if you haven't known."

Private Bamford was anything but a fool and he was an older man and kind. His son was nearly Freddy Mann's age.

"You'll be—they'll be all right, sir." He stopped himself from the awful breach of discipline just in time. "Talk to 'em about it sometimes, I 'ave. Just a word like, cheery." The growl became even more sepulchral and forbidding. "Just one thing there is, I always tell 'em—what we said in South Africa—that's what I always tell 'em. No need to worry, lads, I tells 'em. If yer bullet's got yer number on it then yer for it, and there ain't no dodging. But if it ain't got yer number, it can't get yer, so there ain't no need to worry. It's all a matter o' that—just whether the bullet's got yer number—and thinking or worrying can't change that. That's the way to cheer 'em, sir, you'll find. Just you tell 'em that. Moving off soon, sir, we'll be. No need to worry if the bullet ain't got yer number. That's all there is to it, as the sayin' goes, just whether a bullet's got yer number."

Common soldiers' philosophy—well, he supposed it was about as good as any other, as good as any that had occurred to him during the past few weeks. So long as it worked. That was what one wanted to get hold of, something that would stop a fellow asking the eternal question, stop him from being—no, it wasn't exactly that. It wasn't exactly for himself he minded so much, but he was afraid of appearing to funk it before the men; that would be ghastly, for they would be bound to know. He rather wished he hadn't read that book a month ago at Aldershot—that book *The Four Feathers*, about the fellow who resigned as soon as war broke out. It was that that had set him thinking so, worrying, wondering. How could he tell? What had he had in his life so far except one or two hard games of footer and an occasional bathe in a roughish sea. There was nothing at Edenhurst or at Three Oaks Grammar School at all like this. He smiled a little grimly. Well, here it was; he'd soon know now.

On now down the Menin Road. Robbie was just ahead, imperturbable as usual. The Skipper blew like a grampus up and down the line, with an occasional "Now steady, men. Now look, Mr. Williams; now, Robbie lad." Harry's temper seemed to be getting a little short, but Freddy Mann was soon to learn that this was a peculiarity of Harry's near the line and betokened no ill-will. On now, past the Ecole de Bienfaisance to the White Château, threading their way now through closely packed dark moving figures, with the dark mass of the ramparts, the tower of the Cloth Hall and the flames of Ypres behind them. By this time local knowledge was becoming all-important. "Wouldn't bother with yer map, sir, not if I was you." Freddy Mann heard the company guide remark in a cheerful Cockney voice to the Skipper who was struggling at every halt with prismatic compass and maps of all shapes and sizes. "Them two broken chairs and the dead 'orse's 'ead by the 'edge is where we turn off—them's what yer want to guide yer into West Lane. All very well them maps, but it's things like that yer want to know when there's wire about, same as what yer've got it 'ere. 'Ell Fire Corner, that is," he nodded carelessly in reply to a question. "Straight ahead. Pretty spot, I give yer *my* word. 'Ell of a bloody 'ole, I calls it. We gets into the trench 'ere, sir. Mind the wire. Ain't any use ducking, sir, not from bullets, not if yer outside a trench. Overs, that's all there is. Put yer to sleep if they get yer, but they ain't aimed at yer, so what's the odds. Captain Corra, he said he'd be 'ere to meet us, if all was well up there. I'll just look round and—ah 'ere 'e is. 'Ere's Captain Corra. 'Ere's this 'ere 'C' Company, sir, same as what I fetched."

Private Walley, the guide with the general air of one who had just introduced Stanley to Livingstone, saluted smartly, hitched his rifle on his shoulder, and retired to the lee side of a ruined wall, to await further orders and enjoy a well-earned drink. Freddy Mann looked with interest upon a quite unusually slow-moving and imperturbable individual who emerged from the side of the road to greet the company. He seemed to Freddy Mann's Aldershot-trained mind to be regrettably lacking not only in appreciation of the value of cover, but also in equipment. In contrast to their efficient selves, he carried nothing but a respirator slung across his shoulder and a pistol. Even the pistol he would fain have left behind, but, as he explained apologetically to the "C" Company officers in a dug-out a little later on, you never quite know what you're going to meet in a show like this. His average rate of speech was about thirty words a minute, and Freddy Mann gained the impression that his rate of thought corresponded. He greeted the voluble Skipper with undisturbed sang-froid, and with him walked along the company.

"Thought I'd stroll down to meet you," he explained. "Glad you've come along. Bit quietish here just now, of course, but we'll try to show you a bit of what's going on. Yes, that's it, Railway Wood, that's where we are, bit North of the Menin Road: not a bad sector, so long as the Hun isn't feeling uppish. Might as well be pushing on, I suppose: your fellows ready? Just up these fields to the right and over. Yes, suppose we'd better keep 'em in the trenches, but I usually stroll along the top myself. Wonder what's the matter with the Hun?"

The question might be excused. Suddenly, for no apparent reason, the intermittent shelling behind them became continuous. A new fire had started in Ypres, and flames sprang up in the distance beyond the trees, to throw the skeletons of spires and ruined buildings into darker relief and cast a more livid glow upon the rolling curtain of smoke. "Usual evening hate, I suppose," muttered Captain Corra. "Bit late. Well, it's nothing to do with us. We'll shove along." While the leading platoons were filing man by man from the road, and before it was his turn to move, Freddy Mann watched, half fascinated. So this was to Captain Corra almost an ordinary hate, almost a routine matter.

He hadn't spoken as if to show off, but in an indifferent manner as if he meant it. It probably was a matter of routine to him. Probably it was usual when a battle was going on, but, as Freddy Mann looked about him, the air seemed full of flying steel that he almost imagined that one could see, the crimson sky one sounding board of roaring and crashing thunder. There in Ypres, before it and behind it, flash succeeded flash as the German shells rained down, while lesser stabs appeared from just behind them as the British opened in retaliation. The range of the German shelling was becoming wider: one shell fell in the field to their left, two hundred yards away. They were followed by others, and when at last Freddy Mann moved off it was to the accompaniment, as it appeared to him, of a rising crescendo of flame and fire.

"Livened up a bit," remarked Private Walley, who had joined his platoon unnoticed. "Don't mind if I stroll along with you, sir? The officer has gone up ahead."

"No, please do. Do they often go on like this?"

"Bless you, yes, this ain't nothing. Gets on to Yeeper regular, does the 'Un. Loves it something beautiful. Flies round a 'oney pot ain't in it with the 'Un. Two or three times a day we gets this, Sundays *and* Bank 'Olidays included. Mind yer step 'ere, sir: 'e's a dead 'un, 'e won't move. Don't worry us, that crumping," he pointed over his shoulder to the flames and roar. "Only difficulty is when they starts spreading round like, gets on our front as well. Anything'll start it—bit 'o trench bombing, one of three rounds a day o' our shrapnel, anything of the sort: then away they'll go, on to Yeeper, Brielen, Vlamertinghe, Dickebusch, Kruistraat, Pop itself like as not. Steady 'ere a bit, sir; well, let 'em come up. Can't depend on orders getting down, not with this 'ere bloody row, and we're getting near. Ah, thought so," in rather sobered accents, as he went ahead of Freddy Mann down a shallow C.T. which faced due east. "They've got round into us, the swine. 'Otted up the front; pity, that. Nicer to have got in quiet; we'll just 'ave to go canny. Them damned machine guns, they're at it now."

It appeared impossible to Freddy Mann that there was anything not at it: bullets passed over their heads in a steady stream, or phutted monotonously against the sandbags on the left: the fields ahead of them were lit with Verey lights and flashes, in which odd groups of men, stakes, stumps of trees, and long lines of sandbags showed gaunt for a moment and then were swallowed into a deeper darkness: men groped past or across, laden with duckboards, ration bags, spades, shovels or rolls of wire, cursing softly, feeling their way along the line. Delays seemed interminable, during which there was nothing to do but keep well down to the side of the trench, and hope that all was O.K. behind them and in front.

"Yes, 'e's nasty tonight, is the bloody 'Un. Careful 'ere now, sir: we've got to double this bit, and there's a fixed rifle laid. One at a time, that's it, like them in front: just five yards across this 'ere road, then into that trench and there yer are: just let 'em get across and—ah!"—the dark form in front, just emerged from the trench, gave two steps forward and fell headlong across the parapet. "Got 'im, that 'as," as

Private Walley and Freddy Mann went forward. "Straight through the 'ead, that's got 'im. No, 'tain't no use, sir, 'e's a gonner 'e is——"

"What is it, Bamford?" as Freddy Mann turned from the lifeless body to the burly form that had pressed up along the trench.

"All right, sir—just come to tell yer that—'ullo, Gawd's truth, that ain't Sergeant 'Arris gone?"

Freddy Mann nodded. "First blood to them—that's Harris."

"What 'appened, sir?"

"Sniped, just here at the culvert a moment ago: he was just in front."

Freddy Mann dropped on his knees beside the dying man.

"Quick, Bamford—water—quick. He's——"

The head dropped back.

"No use, sir."

"No use?"

Two pairs of eyes met in the darkness, shining in the sudden glare of an exploding shell.

"No use: it 'ad 'is number." Private Bamford spoke as with the voice of a grim and changeless doom.

CHAPTER IV

IF, as Colonel Steyne, of the 1st Battalion of Loyal Southshires, wisely concluded, you are entrusted with a battalion of inexperienced soldiers and ordered to break them in to it, and accustom them to active service and conditions of trench warfare, it is an excellent idea to get them on to burying. A job like this prevents them from hanging about and crowding the front line trenches; it teaches them to move about a bit in the open and get to know the lie of the land, to keep their eyes skinned for snipers without being told, and to learn above all what a bit of cold mutton looks like and thus to get rid of any squeamish nonsense. There were plenty of dead round Sanctuary Wood and behind Witteport Farm, especially after that last show with the Liverpools, and Colonel Steyne and his brother officer, the C.O. of the Kitchener battalion, agreed that the best thing they could do would be to get on with it and help to clean things up.

Within forty-eight hours, therefore, of their arrival in the Railway Wood sector, "C" Company found themselves well equipped with lime, spades and pickaxes, making their way trenches filled with semi-somnolent or cursing members of their sister battalion and out into the low fields immediately behind the ridge along which the front line ran. There was plenty to do, and the sooner they got on with it the better, as it was a hot day and the corpses stank; there seemed to be about eighty in Freddy Mann's sector alone, some lying separately, some in little groups of three or four, one or two mere skeletons covered with ragged bits of uniform, but most of them in the state of decomposition that one would expect after a month's exposure. Rather pleased at having something to do which, however indirectly, might be considered as helping to win the war, Freddy Mann, after walking round his allotted area with Sergeant Mitchell and Corporal Sugger, who ducked incessantly, talked about South Africa and moved stealthily towards the trenches whenever he could, got his platoon going and found sufficient occupation in siting graves and advising as to the methods and processes of interment. His assistance was in some demand, for there is a peculiar technique attaching to the burying of semi-decomposed bodies under active service conditions, and each case has to be treated, as it were, upon its merits. The chief difficulty arises in regard to the moving of the body to the grave, when dug. Even if it is in one piece when found—and this cannot be assumed—no small degree of skill is often required to preserve its entirety during the process of transfer. A too sudden pull at a boot, and a leg may come off in your hand, as the angry flies rise up around your face. A careful balancing of trunk and limbs upon two spades is sometimes effective, but there is always even then the chance that the head may drop off and roll along, a grisly mass of clotted hair, blackened flesh, maggots, protruding bones and teeth, to come to rest before your feet. Nor does the solution of these problems overcome all difficulties: there remains that question of those little groups, sometimes of three or four, sometimes of two alone, which must either be buried together in an almost shapeless heap, or separated by tearing limb from limb, hand from windpipe, sorted out into what is British and what is German by what signs are still available and laid in pieces, one by one, in due order in separate graves. The thoroughly conscientious member of a burial party will adopt this method, but it takes time, and when the corpses are more closely intertwined and a shell or two has fallen near, there is a temptation to adopt the simpler course. This, for example, was a case in point. Freddy Mann stood for a moment regarding the two bodies which Corporal Garside had asked him to inspect. Thigh to thigh and breast to breast they pressed against each other: behind the neck of one a bayonet stuck out a clear six inches, and the ribs of the other were pierced by the rifle which its owner had pressed downwards with redoubled force when making his headlong plunge. Which, in that welter of maggots and buzzing flies, was the flesh of the Englishman's hand and of the German's throat? Whose were those crooked fingers, lying apparently by themselves beside the pouch? Where was the Englishman's left arm? Come to that, where was the upper part of the German's head? It had to be gone into, and it was not exactly a pleasant job. He felt almost inclined to think, as he bent down, that he'd had about enough of this for one afternoon: the stink seemed if anything to be worse in the clearer evening air. There they lay, gazing at him, those two bloody fools who'd run upon each other's bayonets and expected him to bury them, and they wanted a grave each, he supposed, but what the devil did it matter if . . .

"Hullo! Still at it?"

Freddy Mann looked up and saw by him an officer of middle height, about twenty-five years of age, dark, with stern and clear-cut features, but with a cheerful enough expression. He was standing in a negligent attitude, toying with his pistol and watching the proceedings with an apparently amused interest.

"Hullo—er——"

"Harvey—you know Harvey—that's me—met you at B.H.Q. last night. First Battalion—God's own. How's things?"

"Yes—er—I remember." Freddy Mann straightened himself and paused a moment. "Is there——?"

"No." George Harvey anticipated the question. "Nothing I want. Just strolled out to see how things were going. Nothing to do for an hour or so. Going on patrol tonight, so I thought I'd just stretch my legs. Pleasant job."

He looked round.

"Got some of 'em cleared up, anyway. Good thing, that. We wanted 'em out of the way. Bit of a set-to, these two seem to have had." He nodded his head indifferently towards the rotting and twisted corpses. "Got each other

fair, they did. May 25th show, that was. Bols' crowd.
Fusiliers. Most of 'em got scuppered then. Don't wonder.
Of all the bloody awful shows. What yer going to do with
them?"

"Just wondering, matter of fact. Toler says bury them
separately when possible, but——"

"Shove 'em in together, if I were you. 'In death they were
not divided,' you know. Make it up between 'em, they will,
when they're pushing daisies. Yes, poor swine, they got
their packet. Wonder we didn't, all of us."

"Were you there?"

George Harvey nodded.

"In with Bols, our crowd. Came up from Flammers in
the afternoon, and struck it fair. Shoved off at 12, left our
dinners on the boil, got along God knows how to G.H.Q.
line—you know—that bit along by Hell Fire Corner—got
tied up in the wire there waiting for the Suffolks, then
pushed up to Witteport and waited for the 80th. 80th
came along about midnight, bless their hearts, dropping
fellows all the way: 500 odd they dropped that day.
However, they got here, cursing like mad, and we all got
settled in, linked up with the Cavalry in Zouave Wood,
dug in all nice and comfortable and happy, and here we
are. Devil of a show that was: close call, if ever there was
one: sort of thing we're always having here. Damned
thankful, this city ought to be to us. When I think of what
I've done for Wipers——"

He waved a hand toward the towers of Ypres, now
tinged with the setting sun.

It was difficult, Freddy Mann thought, to know how far to take him seriously. He spoke always with that slightly cynical smile, but rather grim expression.

"You've seen a good deal here then?"

"Most of it, old son. Here or hereabouts, on or off all the time since October. Good shooting season, if ever there was one. All the time just hanging on. And we were told when we got here we were going through to Menin."

He laughed, as he squatted on a little hillock on the ground.

"That feller"—he pointed to a skeleton—"he probably thought he was going through to Menin. He was one of October's lot by the look of him. But most of 'em learnt their mistake over there—round there by Gheluvelt and Polygon Wood. That's where they learnt, October 31st. We were practically done that day. The Worcesters, they were all that saved us. Lanax himself thought we were done. God knows how we hung on."

"What was it like?" The question, Freddy Mann knew, was a schoolboy question, doubly ridiculous when asked as now, within a few hundred yards from the German lines. But it was peaceful now in comparison. Harvey had seen the flames of war.

"What was it like? Like—oh, hell—you'll know one day, soon enough probably—like anything else in this blasted war. No reserves—that was what was the matter there. Brigadiers in shell holes, just behind the line. Cooks in the firing line. Horses' heads flying all over the place and no guns or shells; you know—the ordinary sort of thing—what it always is like—been like ever since. Just the same last month, with gas thrown in. And we've lost a lot of ground since then. Decent city, Wipers was, in those merry days; drinks about and things. Damned poor place now."

"Why do we keep it?—that's what I can't understand. This Salient——"

"You aren't the first to ask that, old son," said George Harvey cheerfully. "And I don't suppose you'll be the last. Some say it's to keep the Belgians in, some say because G.H.Q. don't know we're here, or it's the only place they've got maps of. All I know is we do, and it's damned well time you fellers came out to help us."

"Wasn't our fault we didn't come before."

"No, and I'll believe that." George Harvey got up and placed his hand on Freddy Mann's shoulder with a kindly smile. "And you're young enough now, seems to me, some of you. How old are you?"

"Nineteen. Left school last July."

"Mm." George Harvey grunted. "Bit of a change to this. You——" He looked warmly at Freddy Mann, then stopped. "Good chaps, your chaps, what I've seen of them. Harry, he's one of the best. And Robbie, that's a chap I like. Doesn't talk. That's the sort."

He looked towards Robinson, quietly supervising and helping his burial party in the adjacent field.

"Glad you've come, you know. It's bucked our fellows up, all this 'K.1' business. Suppose you've come out to do the trick."

"Well, anyway, to win the war."

39

George Harvey nodded, but the smile was hardly visible this time. He looked towards Ypres, and Freddy Mann followed his gaze.

"That's all we've done so far, save Ypres. We talked like that, last year. September 10th I crossed. But that's all we've done so far. Nine months—that's all there is to show."

He paused. The twilight was coming on, and the stumps of trees and towers were beginning to get indistinct in the distance. An occasional early starlight rose and fell.

"Damned big, you know, this war. In England you see it as a whole. Here it's only little bits. This bit, for example, that's all I know. And all these fellows," he pointed to the unburied dead, and the graves of those just buried. "All they'll ever know. Stands for a lot does Ypres. Devil of a lot to the Southshires, anyway. He hasn't got it yet, the Hun, and he's tried damned hard. This job, for example—it was touch and go."

He pointed to where the German bullet-proof shelters faced Ypres on the reverse side of the trench near where they were standing.

"See that?"

Freddy Mann nodded.

"You know what that means?"

"Yes."

"Damned near, I tell you. Just those fields, then there's Ypres. And the Boche was in this trench."

He looked again at the huddled mass at their feet, for which Corporal Garside and his men were digging their common grave.

"He was hanging on, that feller. Straight through the throat he got him. Never a dog's chance, either of 'em. Well, anyway, he didn't win the war, but he was doing something hanging on."

The night was falling. Nights at Ypres were ghostly.

"Better pack up now and get along. I've got to shove off to this patrol. Bit chippy now. Come and have a tot to keep the cold out. May come again tonight, the Hun, for all I know. But it's safe so far, is Wipers. It's a rum place, Ypres. Come on!"

He moved a few steps, laughed a trifle nervously, and nodded to the corpses.

"Come on. Those fellers'll stay on guard."

CHAPTER V

STAND-TO. So far, all O.K., but they'd had a lively time. They'd only got into the line the previous night, and the Colonel, the Skipper, and the German artillery and snipers hadn't given them much peace since they arrived. He himself had done what he could within the time. He'd been round his three dug-outs and two sapheads and got his sentries posted and reliefs told off, and he'd found the way to B.H.Q. in Cambridge Road, which wanted a little doing in itself, and he'd managed to get a look at his wire from No Man's Land. That was the great thing, as Townroe was always ramming down their throats at Aldershot, and those fellows of the 1st Battalion—get out into No Man's Land at all costs, and see for yourself what things are like. Judging from the time he'd spent there, assing about with Robbie in front of their platoon sectors, it wasn't a particularly cheerful place, and he didn't seem to have done much there except tread on the stomach of a dead Boche, lose his prismatic compass and get his hand half bitten off by a rat about the size of a full-grown rabbit that came up to him as he was lying "doggo" in the grass. Still, he'd been there, not this time as a novitiate in training, but in his own right as officer commanding that sector of the front. Sixty yards from the corner of Railway

Wood to Witteport Farm he held that night, and so far he'd held it safe. That, it seemed to him, was doing the thing that mattered. Nothing in front. He raised himself a fraction to peer through the mists that lay heavy upon the fields towards a jagged line of stakes just discernible in the fading moon: nothing in front but those armed forces which to him and those with him must needs stand as the powers of death and evil. And there, with Ypres and the sea behind them, he and his platoon were stationed, with a job, the nature of which he understood, to do. Robbie was on one side of him, Malcolm upon the other, and beyond them on either side the vast curve of the British line bent almost upon itself round Ypres. And round the rim of that tortured curve and beyond it, to the marshes in the north and the mountains in the south, men were ranged as they were ranged here, bayonets pointing to the east, ready for what the dawn might bring. As at Railway Wood, so at Boesinghe or Hill 60 or La Bassée or Verdun or the Vosges, men were sweating blood, sniping and being sniped, prowling like starving beasts of prey, and occasionally from the hours of darkness plucking some curious moments of an unexpected peace. Here at least the night was quiet now, as it gave place to the coming day: star shells still flickered unevenly, but the dawn was breaking fast; fields and farms were more distinct, and beyond the trees the towers of Ypres had already caught the rays of the early sun. That first night of straining vigil was nearly over; dusk changed to grey; the mists began to lift along the fields, and behind them at last Ypres stood clear in the light of morning against the sky. "Stand down": a sniper's rifle cracked, and the day of warfare had begun again. But the night was over, and so far he had not betrayed his trust.

CHAPTER VI

"SOLDIERING," remarked Private Bamford, as he turned a heavy eye upon the other occupants of the dugout and slowly rolled and lit a cigarette. "This 'ere soldiering ain't what it used to be."

Private Derek Rossiter, ex-undergraduate of Trinity, put down his pencil and leaned forward with interest. "To what in particular do you take exception?"

"Eh?"

"What's the matter with the bloody war?" in the same well-bred, even tones.

"You'd know, Mr. Rossiter, if you'd seen South Africa."

" 'Is name's Brains," from the irresponsible Bartlett. "Go on."

"I knows respect, me lad, where respect is due. And that's more than can be said for some. Well, in South Africa," he continued, "we soldiered proper. But 'ere, for a month we've been in this bloody country with this 'ere battalion, and not one bloomin' Boche 'ave I or any of us seen. Crawling up and down these trenches, living in these 'ere dug-outs, keeping your buttons and yer side arms dirty—that ain't soldiering. Look at the officers, too—I asks yer, look at them."

"What's the matter with 'em?" from the mild, middle-aged, and evidently much married Private Beard. "Nice well-spoken cheery lot. Bit wild at times, but most of 'em ain't married. None the worse for that."

"That's as may be, but where's their swords? Married or not, an officer ought to wear 'is sword. 'Ow can yer 'ave discipline if officers don't carry swords? Tunics, too. Captain 'Arry 'e's taken to wearing a Tommy's tunic in the trenches—dirty one at that. My officer 'e talked o' doing the same, but I told 'im it wouldn't do. All wrong, all this 'ere mix-up, yer know, in this 'ere 'K.1.' And there's officers ought to be in the ranks, and fellers in the ranks that should be officers—same as you, Mr. Rossiter. It's all of a piece, seems to me—all mixed up. To 'ave fellers in the ranks talkin' same as you do, it ain't in accord with army ways."

"Suppose not. But this is a new army and a new war, you know. This, my venerable Denis, is the war for civilisation, the war to end war, as our martial Skipper has told us with such verbal embellishment. New wine in old bottles—you know." Rossiter took up his pencil again.

Private Bartlett whistled. "That's talk, that is. Lumme, Brains, yer can't 'arf talk. That's got yer, grandpa. Ain't got much, I'll lay, to say to that."

Private Bamford looked a little helpless for a moment.

" 'Tain't I'm growsing, exactly."

He paused a moment.

"All this talk, for example—look at that. Talk about winnin' the war, yer know, and all that sort of thing. It's unsettling. Course we wants to win the war, but we wants to do it quiet like and natural. Ought to 'ear what some of them 1st Battalion fellers are sayin' about the way our fellers are foolin' about in this 'ere sector—chucking bombs about, crumpin' when there ain't no need to crump, mucking up the line generally. Captain Corra, 'e warn't too pleased."

"Ah, he should welcome our enthusiasm."

"P'raps he should, but 'e don't. Takes the war as it comes, 'e does, and goes along quiet with his job. Look at 'im and then at the Skipper, volunteering for this, suggesting that, looking round for trouble generally. Take that sap-'ead business on Tuesday, when we all of us nearly stopped a packet—that was due to 'im."

Private Beard nodded approvingly.

"You're right there. Pity to spoil a bit o' quiet when yer've got it. 'Tain't too easy not to get a bit o' quiet in life. But I suppose——"

He looked round.

"Some of us was volunteers, you know. This ain't our job. Me, for example. Shopkeeper I am, same as I've often told you—little shop down Bethnal Green. Suppose I came out—to 'elp to win the war. That's what 'appened with most of us. Look at Brains 'ere. Look at the officers. 'Ardly one of 'em knew a rifle from a walkin' stick a year ago. Sammy, 'e's a singer, and Duff, 'e's an artist, and——"

Private Bamford in his turn nodded agreement.

"That's what it is, old cock, and it makes it 'ard for soldiering. Excitable sort of ideas, these fellers get. If yer go about singing and painting and such, yer bound to get excited. Spreads, too. Same as my officer. Nice quiet little chap 'e is, but look at 'im yesterday after stand-to. Started when I brought 'is rations. Started talking just like them others, worse if anything—winning the war for 'umanity, and the glory of Yeeper. Glory of Yeeper—I asks yer"—as Private Bamford lifted a baleful eye. "What can yer make o' that?"

"Glory of Yeeper—ah, 'e ain't the only one at that game. There's Brains 'ere. Come on Brains, let's show 'em," as Private Bartlett darted up and seized a paper from Rossiter's side. "Look at this," as he thrust it into the other's hand. "Brains wrote this. Last week 'e wrote it and sent it 'ome, and 'ere it is in print, and 'is initials, too. You read that, granddad. That'll do yer good. Make yer think."

Slightly puzzled, Private Bamford took the paper, looked at the title of a poem, at the initials "D. R." beneath, crossed his legs, put a pipe into the corner of his mouth, laid his forefinger carefully upon the first line and read:

"Fair was your City, old and fair,
  And fair the Hall where the kings abode;
 And you speak to us in your despair—
 To us, who see but ruins bare,
 A shattered wall, a broken stair,
  And graves on the Menin Road.

"It was sweet, you say, from the city wall
  To watch the fields where the horsemen rode;
 It was sweet to hear at evenfall
 Across the moat the voices call;
 It was good to see the stately hall
  From the fields by the Menin Road.

48

"Yea, citizens of the City Dead,
*   Whose souls are torn by memory's goad;*
* But now there are stones in the old Hall's stead,*
* And the moat that you loved is sometimes red,*
And echoes are stilled and laughter sped,
*   And torn is the Menin Road.*

"And by the farms and the House of White,
*   And the shrine where the little candles glowed,*
There is silence now by day and night,
Or the sudden crash and the blinding light,
For the guns smite ever as thunders smite,
*   And there's Death on the Menin Road."*

He looked up and out of the dug-out entrance to a haze of smoke that lay above the bare stumps of trees behind them, then back at Rossiter, apparently indifferent, clear-cut of face, athletic of body, one who had already proved in action those qualities which one felt instinctively in his case there was no need to prove, then back to the page again.

"Fair was your City, old and fair."

"You wrote that, Mr. Rossiter?"

"I'm afraid I did."

"Then yer knows 'ow to put these 'ere words into poetry same as this."

"Sometimes."

"And—yer in the ranks."

"Apparently."

Private Bamford remained thoughtful for a full fifteen seconds. At last he opened his mouth and spoke.

"It's a rum thing, this 'ere war, and there's rum things in it." He looked at the page again. "And yer tell me yer wrote them words?"

"I was the servant of the Muse: the spirit moved me and I wrote."

"Whaffor—yer ain't enjoyin' it by any chance?"

"Can't say that I am—and yet——"

" 'Tain't natural not to talk like that. But it's all of a piece, me lad, same as what I tell yer. Took the Army quiet like, we did, same as it ought to be took. But soldiering, it ain't what it used to be."

CHAPTER VII

FREDDY MANN spoke little as he led his platoon out of the Lille Gate, across the bridge and along the railway embankment to the south of Ypres. He had indeed sufficient reason for reflection. The R.E. Major had no doubt meant well enough: he was a jovial sort, and it was just his way; but it did seem that to send him and his party forth from the ramparts with a cheery final remark to the effect that the Boche had been shelling the site of the machine gun emplacement which they had to build all day, and "he didn't suppose that any of them would return alive" was not on the whole in the best of taste. It was all very well to joke about it when he was going off to a cheery dinner at the Goldfish Château, but what about the fellow who with this parting blessing in his ears had to do the job? The R.E. Corporal, too, didn't make things any easier. Though Freddy Mann did not yet realise it, the lordly air of an R.E. corporal has been known to subdue even junior staff officers and regimental officers under field rank. Corporal Bonner held himself and his profession in due regard, and had sound views upon the correct relationship between the R.E. and the infantry, more particularly between "K.1" and a time-serving out-since-Mons N.C.O. like himself. He spoke at intervals, but his remarks were hardly calculated to dissipate the prevailing gloom. He quite agreed that it was a nasty spot that they were going to, and he bore out the Major's statement by observing in more general terms that it was shelled all day and most of the night. No, it wasn't a particularly easy place to find, because once you passed Birr Cross Roads it was just as easy to wander into the Boche lines as your own; they would have to note the way rather carefully, as he was afraid that he wouldn't be there to guide them back, since he had various other jobs to do, after he had got them settled down. Well, it was a bit difficult to say exactly what one ought to do if casualties occurred. You couldn't leave them alone, of course, as a man didn't have a dog's chance there when once he was hit; you couldn't, on the other hand, spare men to look after them. This machine gun emplacement had to be built tonight at any cost, as the Corps Commander himself demanded to know that it was completed by the following day; it would be a five-hours' job at least, and they wouldn't be there till 10. On the other hand, if they didn't get away by 3 they wouldn't get away at all, as a fly couldn't move there without being seen by daylight. After half an hour of this sort of thing, Freddy Mann gave up fruitless attempts to derive consolation from Corporal Bonner, and began to reflect for himself upon the brighter aspects of the situation. After all, he'd had three or four working parties before this during the last ten days. This was in rather a sticky sector, but it made no real difference; things hardly ever did go wrong on working parties, even in sticky sectors, simply because the Hun was always at the same game as well. So far, nobody could reasonably find fault with the night. Oxford

Street seemed a very reasonably adequate sort of trench, and, most important, he had his own fellows with him as well, which was a damned sight better than taking out Bill's or Sammy's crowd, or those paralytics of "B" Company, as he had had to do last week. They were all there, all the Badajos Barracks fellows, except poor Leader and Downton. They were shoving apparently happy enough along the trench behind him, Bamford, just in his rear, breathing as usual like a steam engine and growling to himself, Beard tugging at his unkempt little sandy moustache and probably discussing his hopeful's whooping cough or mumps with any who would listen, hard nuts like Bettson or the ex-navvy Scrott, Brains, almost certainly pouring forth epigrams and carrying somebody else's sandbags as well as his own, pale-faced little Barton, Corporal Sugger—near enough to the side of the trench and knees well bent, if he knew anything of Corporal Sugger—and bringing up the rear the fatherly, mild-voiced Sergeant Mitchell. Then again, and this in itself made up for a multitude of ills, behind his contingent there was Robbie with most of the rest of the company. On the whole, then— be damned to this R.E. fool, as Freddy Mann looked with a sudden access of confidence towards Corporal Bonner: Birr Cross Roads, was it, and it was tricky going after this? He'd better get on with it, then, and not talk quite so much, and be damned to all his croaking for an old wives' tale.

"This is where they've been getting on to it—all round 'ere," Corporal Bonner nodded towards a welter of new shell holes, from which a strong earthy smell arose, and lines of broken sandbags facing them in the moonlight along the ridge past the culvert. "All about 'ere; it's a twisty bit, and, as I say, you'll need to mark yer way."

"Right: shove on." Now that Oxford Street was left behind them Freddy Mann was experiencing a strong feeling that he was embarking upon an enchanted sea, but he was giving nothing away. Occasionally, from some tumbled dug-out, a head or two appeared, but otherwise nothing moved save grass and rats. After a time signs of other inhabitants ceased to appear, and they crept alone, and very stealthily, through a maze of wire, shell-holes and ruined trenches to their destination. Lucky it was a quiet night. They were near the plateau at last, and just over there, behind the wire, was the Boche: here were the tapes all ready laid for the embankment, so now tunics off and down to it, and for God's sake see that nobody makes a noise. Nothing to worry about, of course, but it's a bit on the near side, and there's nobody else about, and—it was a damned silly remark for the Major to have made.

•　　•　　•　　•　　•

Pity about this. The Major had done his best for them, and it wasn't his fault that no shell had fallen and hardly a rifle or machine gun had been heard since ten o'clock, that the men had got started without any trouble, and that now, at 2.30, the job was practically done. They'd done it pretty well on their own, too: an R.E. corporal in attendance upon an infantry working party usually has about as many other jobs as a porter at a terminus on a

Bank Holiday, and as far as they were concerned Corporal Bonner hadn't done as much as Private Bamford. Not that on this occasion such a comparison conveyed as much as would usually have been the case, for Private Bamford had got into the job tonight. Freddy Mann for once had taken no chances: he had turned a deaf ear to Bamford's representations as to the importance of an officer's comfort, and his batman had dug his little sector with the rest of them; furthermore, he and his comrades, knowing exactly where they were in relation to the enemy, had not tarried in the digging. No, it wasn't the R.E.'s fault that things had gone well that night, that they had had no casualties, that in four hours a machine gun emplacement had been completed that would satisfy the most exacting of corps commanders; no fault of theirs that at about 1 p.m. he and Robbie, knowing that the situation was now in hand, had had an unforgettable moment during the midway easy, lying on their backs concealed in the rank grasses of untilled fields, and watching the starlights flicker and fall against the clear sky of the summer night, till suddenly, here at Hooge, on the roof of an unknown world, a strange spirit of utter and elemental peace had touched them. No fault, all this, of the Major's, and, by Jove! they'd let him know. Back now, tails up, down past the Culvert to the Birr Cross Roads, past Gordon Farm and the Halfway House, back to the embankment and the gates of Ypres. Mitchell and Baines could take the men up those few hundred yards to the Prison, while he and Robbie dug out the Major to tell him all about it; it was high time he was about at 5 a.m. and they were certain he would like to know that the job was done. The Major looked at them with interest. Full of it, weren't they, this curly-headed boy and this quietly elated sober-faced young man; thought they'd won the war to all intents and purposes, if one could judge from the way they talked. Well, well—the Major stuck his hands deeper into the pockets of his British warm, looked at them and smiled.

"Think you've done down Hooge, eh? Think you're top dog over Wipers? Think again, young feller-me-lads. All right this time, I grant you, but—have a drink and think again."

CHAPTER VIII

T HIS was as it should be: there was peace in Ypres tonight. Major Baggallay walked contentedly, humming to himself as he smoked a cigarette and strolled along the middle of the road. He was a wily old war-dog, and he knew his Ypres. They wouldn't shell Ypres again tonight. Funny thing, that, about Ypres: you might have hell let loose the whole day long, and then about six or seven o'clock it would all die down and you could shove along the Menin Road with the reliefs, or stroll about by the Cloth Hall, as if you were in Piccadilly. Today was a case in point—nothing but 8.9s all the morning, and Jack Johnsons from 2 to 5; beast of a day it had been, but it had all stopped at 7, and he'd got along to the "C" Company Mess without hearing a crump from the Ramparts to the Lille Gate. Jolly good thing it was so, as it was only that that made Ypres possible. Ypres—he knew a bit about war, he did, after the Sudan and South Africa, but he'd never struck anything quite like this. It was no use pretending even with these kids in "K.1" that he was used to it; he felt the strain as much as anybody, even if he knew too much about the game to show it. He wasn't sure really that he didn't feel it rather more. They were good chaps in this battalion, O.K. so far in the line, but God, they weren't half

57

kids! That "C" Company mess this evening, for example. They'd done him well enough, no complaints on that score, in spite of old Toler's sideways looks as the whisky went round, but they were just like a party of schoolboys who'd suddenly struck casualties on a field day on Salisbury Plain. Well, not Harry perhaps. Harry was a tough nut who didn't talk much in the line except to damn his sergeant-major, and didn't buck too much about the war. But the rest, except old go-to-prayer-meeting Toler, were kids enough—that young blighter Jack, with his tales of windjamming round Cape Horn, and that cheery Scotch giant Malcolm, and Robbie, and Freddy Mann. Good pair, that pair, all the same; sort of—who were the Johnnies— oh, yes, Achilles and Patroclus they seemed to be. Lucky swine, Freddy Mann, to have a friend like Robbie. He'd told Townroe more than once that he was the one absolute thoroughbred in the battalion. Pale, quiet fellow he was, but he'd never seen him wilt. Always out and about at the hottest corner, pulling away at his pipe, doing stunts that he never said anything about, knew his men backwards, hard as nails—there wasn't much the matter with Oxford if it still turned out chaps like that. And Freddy Mann, the "Cherub," he had the right stuff in him, but he was green to a degree, the "Cherub." Everything seemed to surprise him—an old soldier's wish for a Blighty, the effects of rum, the morals of majors at the base, that poor swine Garton's death from heart failure, Army sergeants and their pretty little ways—he seemed to have come from the cradle straight to Ypres. Rum thing, life, for a fellow like the "Cherub." Little country grammar school, vicar's tea parties, a day excursion or two to London, which seemed to have been his greatest delight this time last year, leaves school, goes into the local bank, just starts smoking and having a latchkey of his own, then this.

The Major paused as he turned at the corner of the Rue de Lille, opposite the Cloth Hall, to the right towards the Ramparts. Peaceful enough—just that one house blazing away behind the cathedral—but, God, how big! They didn't know, poor kids, how big. Perhaps they believed all wars were the same as this. But he—he'd soldiered for thirty years, and this was something that he'd never known before. Any one of these nights and days would have meant a battle and a medal upon the sands of Egypt. What was Roorke's Drift compared to an outpost show at Hooge, with trench mortars and minnies raising living hell, and gas for all they knew coming down upon the wind? They'd thought a lot of themselves when they'd managed to hold Ladysmith, but what was Ladysmith to Ypres? A few potty guns a mile or two away, a few odd snipers, fifty casualties a week or so, and here in layer on layer around them were a thousand guns, divisions massed upon divisions, hungry to advance and thrust them from Ypres to Poperinghe, Pop to Hazebrouck, Hazebrouck to the sea, while as for casualties—that, if any, was the part of his job at B.H.Q. he mostly loathed. It got on his nerves, that daily toll. "Killed in action and struck off strength"; section by section, company by company, they'd paid their price, and nothing to show for it but Ypres. Ypres—yes, by God, he hated Ypres.

Talk about human sacrifice—why that Cloth Hall itself was like a jagged tooth, looking as if it might belong to some beast that just wanted to go on swallowing flesh and blood. What were the casualties now within the Salient—10,000, 20,000, 30,000—what did it matter? It seemed as if it would go on like this for ever now, in and out Vlamertinghe, Ypres, Railway Wood, Hooge—it was only a few weeks, but it had been long enough.

Well, war was his job, he supposed, as he stumped across the square. He'd chosen it, and it wasn't up to him to grizzle, but he was 58 and he was tired. He felt a bit past this sort of thing. Game for the young, this game. He'd laughed at his wife, when she'd tried to stop one more old dug-out joining up at York, and he'd managed to carry through so far, but he was tired. He was an old man, and it was a bit beyond him; it was big and new. Freddy Mann— why his younger son was older than Freddy Mann—more like his grandson almost, with his cheeks and mop of curly hair; it was their show, after all, not his. The garden at Ilkley, that's where he ought to be; it came to his mind, that garden on a peaceful night like this. Keep safe, she'd said, when he packed up and shoved along. He'd never shown the feather in thirty years, nor asked for safety, but he couldn't help just thinking of it now. He was ready for it still, ready as Tom with the Grand Seas Fleet, or Derek at the Dardanelles, but he was old, damned old, and he was glad that just tonight he would sleep in peace. Here was his tunnel in the ramparts. He looked into the black mouth and up to the solid earth above. Forty feet of soil above his head; the shell was not yet made that would break through forty feet. Tomorrow he'd be ready for it all again, ready with the best, but tonight he'd just forget and sleep in peace. Damned dark, this tunnel, and deep. Here was old Parker; better not wake him. Hard on a dark night to find his way about inside. So much the better—there would be peace tonight.

But at that tunnel in the ramparts a definite advance in twentieth-century artillery practice was made that night. The next morning daylight poured through a channel of forty feet into a twisted mass of masonry, broken timber, bones and spattered blood. Portions of four dead men were strewn around. There was no mark or wound upon the Major; but in spirit he was with those others, and a peace had come upon him that was deeper than the peace he asked.

CHAPTER IX

"DON'T think he's shamming, not meself I don't. Can't tell, yer know; but if you was to ask me, I wouldn't call it shamming."

Tom Bamford and Willy Beard sat each in his corner of the dug-out. Willy Beard leaned forward, hands on knees, as he spoke, and regarded the man on the floor with his head on one side and a puzzled expression on his face.

"Say it came on sudden, do yer, Dick?"

"Yes." Dick Bartlett looked up, his arm still round Private Garton's neck. "Sudden like it came on; he was all right afore; just as we was coming along that sap-'ead, out towards Y Wood. 'Ere, 'old up, mate." He leaned down again and put his arm round Garton's back to support him during a sudden burst of vomiting and coughing. " 'Ere, Bett, got yer water-bottle on yer? P'raps 'e wants a drink."

"Sometimes they does it by swallowing soap or something of the sort. 'Ere y'are." Private Bettson handed over his water-bottle with his usual expression of resigned gloom. "Some of the reg'lars does it—scrimshankin', that's what it's called. Didn't 'ave no soap about 'im, yer didn't notice?"

"Not that I knows of—'e ain't that sort. 'Appened sudden like, that's the funny thing about it. Just shoving along the trench we was, time they was crumping a bit this afternoon——"

"Yes—remember that." Beard nodded. " 'Eard 'em round about two o'clock, Y Wood way. Thought yer might be gettin' it."

"That's it. Bit 'eavy it was, usual sort of stuff. Then one comes pretty near; then all of a sudden 'e falls about and starts this game. Don't seem to be 'it nowhere, that's the funny thing about it."

Private Bartlett fingered Garton's back and legs. "Ain't no blood, not that I can see. Often a bad sign, though, when there ain't no blood. What d'yer make of it, Tom?"

"Damned 'ard to say. If it was in South Africa now, I'd 'ave called it 'eat-stroke. In South Africa——"

"Damn South Africa." Private Bettson turned round with a savage growl. "You and yer bloody snowballin' in South Africa. This blasted shellin', that's what it is in my opinion—there you are, they're at it again. Railway Wood, that is. That's it, those field-guns of ours, that's what it is— they always starts it."

Private Bettson looked round.

"What the 'ell's the use of their bangin' off the way they do? Three rounds a day, that's all they got, an' they poops 'em off, and this is what we gets for it. Four bloody 'ours of it today alone."

"They was shelling Vlamertinghe this afternoon." The peaceful Beard usually bore out the remarks of the last speaker. " 'E doesn't look so well, not now 'e don't. Kid o' mine, 'e was taken once like that. Ever tell yer"—he turned to Bamford—"about that kid o' mine?"

"Yes." Tom Bamford was watching Garton more intently. "Don't like that blue around 'is lips, yer know. 'Ere's the bloody Corporal," under his breath, as the dug-out entrance darkened and Corporal Sugger appeared.

"What's all this?" said Corporal Sugger, his underlip protruding under his short black moustache. "Where's the feller? 'Ere, you get up," as he gave Private Garton a kick.

" 'Ere, steady, mate."

"Who the 'ell are you, matin' me? Wounded or shammin', that's what I want to know. Come on, yer bastards, 'as he got 'it or not?"

"No, leastways not that we can see, but——"

"Then 'e's shammin'. Bound to get it, with you fellers— always said so. Y'ain't soldiers—that's what it is. Get up."

Another kick.

Private Garton moved restlessly.

"Never you mind 'is mouth." Corporal Sugger turned to Bartlett, who was wiping some foam from his lips. "That's an old trick, that is—like spitting blood: don't take me in, that don't."

"P'raps not, Corporal, but if 'e can't move 'e can't."

"You keep yer bloody mouth shut, or you'll be for it, too." Corporal Sugger turned with an added ferocity to his arch enemy, Private Bamford. " 'Ave you before the officer."

"Well, now, I wonder? Seems to me yer'd better get the officer, or doctor, or something; 'tain't as if we was gettin' any further. Look at 'im now."

Private Garton's breathing was becoming more laboured. His hands clasped and unclasped spasmodically.

"Easy enough put on, that is. However"—Corporal Sugger paused a moment—"soon fix 'im, I will. 'Ere, Bettson, you get Trott."

The dressing station was near, and within a few minutes the M.O. had taken charge of the case. A talkative fellow, the M.O., a fellow who believed in jollying things up, in putting a cheerful face upon it, in keeping up one's pecker, in not giving way.

"That's it, me lad, soon have you on yer feet. Let's just feel, here and here. Ah yes, nothing broken—not even scratched as far as I can see. Let's have a look at his mouth—no, that foam's nothing—yes—well——" He rapidly slipped a capsule between Private Garton's lips. "That'll buck you up. Feel better now, lad? Yes, that's right."

Private Garton had struggled to a sitting position and was looking round.

"That's it—that's right." A hearty smack upon the back assisted the patient to a more erect posture. "Just keep on like that. Give him a drink of tea—no rum. Got a stretcher case or two, but I'll be back in half an hour. No, Corporal, he's not shamming—just a touch of shock—plenty like that. There's worse things happen at sea. See you soon. Just jolly him up a bit—that's all he wants."

"Told yer 'e wasn't shammin'. Thank Gawd the Corporal's gone," as the dug-out breathed again. "Ought to 'ave known, too, 'cos what Sugger doesn't know o' scrimshankin'—Gawd, there 'e's off again. 'Ere, mate, I don't like this," as Bartlett turned to Beard. "Get Trott back."

The M.O. had unfortunately decided to jolly up the front-line trenches. Private Beard found the dressing station empty, while the others watched round a scarcely breathing figure.

"Can't 'e get the Corporal or something?" Bartlett muttered anxiously. " 'Ere, mate, 'ave a drink o' tea. Rub 'is 'ands, Bet—'e seems all cold."

"It's all this bloody shellin'. Wish to Gawd they'd stop. Oh, Gawd, that was near."

"Rub 'is 'ands, yer fool." Bartlett shouted to Bettson above the crashes, "Thank Gawd, 'ere's the officer. It's Private Garton, sir; very queer he is, sir. Get inside, sir, quick."

"Damned nearly on us. That's in the next trench." Freddy Mann dived into the dug-out. "Fit, is it?"

"Looks like it. The M.O.'s been, but he's been took worse since."

Freddy Mann looked at the motionless figure.

"Got a glass?"

"Whaffor, sir? 'Ere y'are—'ere's Brain's mirror. This'll do. 'Tain't that, is it?"

"Just hold him. We'll know in a minute. Can you feel his heart?"

"No."

"His 'ands is very cold, sir."

"Can you feel his heart?"

"No." Private Bamford bent lower.

"Like ice, sir, 'is 'ands. Oh, Gawd, this shellin'."

"No sign?"

Private Bamford shook his head.

"All limp, sir, he seems to be."

A minute passed. Freddy Mann took the glass away from the foam-flecked mouth. He examined it carefully at the dug-out entrance.

" 'E's cold all over, sir—'E's——"

"Put a coat over him and shut his eyes. What do you want, Corporal?"

"Just looked in to see that scrimshanker—oh——" Corporal Sugger paused.

"Dead, is 'e?"

"Yes."

He took a step forward and looked at the officer and the men.

"What did he die of?"

"Joy at seeing yer, yer bastard," muttered Bettson. The incessant crashes prevented the words from being heard. "How are we to know? He's dead, that's all. You'd better get a stretcher."

But Corporal Sugger stood motionless, looking at the body.

" 'Ow the 'ell was I to know 'e wasn't shamming? Easy enough. 'Ow was I to know?"

●　　　●　　　●　　　●　　　●

This was what he'd been waiting for. What the devil did the rain matter? Bill stood outside his dug-out, examining his revolver and adjusting the string of his smoke helmet. The worse the weather, the better for the raid: the Hun wouldn't expect them on a night like this. It was about time it came off, about time somebody did something. Hanging about in Railway Wood and being whizz-banged in Cambridge Road wouldn't win the war. If other fellows, like those fellows in the 1st Battalion, were content to sit and smoke, well he wasn't. Devil of a job he'd had, though, to get the Skipper to agree, and then there'd been all the excitement with the Colonel and the Brigadier, and all the reams of orders and instructions. There was too much talk altogether in this war: why not get on with it, and cut out all the quack? Just a few good chaps like Robbie and Freddy Mann and Jack Malcolm: all they wanted to do was to leave it to them, and they'd soon get it through. He'd know all about it, the pretty Hun, before a few more hours were over. He'd know. Bill got up on the firestep, and peered through the line of stakes into the darkness. There they were, tucked away. Let him get at them, that was all. He'd lived for this long enough—dreamed of it, ever since he'd first joined up. Gad, life wasn't half worth living with a job like this in hand. Here were Freddy Mann and Robbie, and the Skipper was round there waiting. Now they'd show 'em. Bill laughed aloud as he gave a final hitch to his equipment, and swung through the driving rain along the trench.

CHAPTER X

"ANY news of the raid?" Private Beard looked up as Dick Bartlett entered, shook the water from his hat and wrung out the bottom of his tunic.

"None I've heard of. Where the 'ell's my rations? 'Ere, Bett, you swine, you've bagged my bully beef."

"Tell yer I ain't—your tin's over there. 'Ave this, too, if yer wants it. Ain't they got nothing but this 'ere bloody bully beef?"

"And can't you do nothing but grouse about yer grub? Damned sight more than yer ever got when yer was down Limehouse, I'll be bound. Chuck over the opener, Beard, old son."

"Better if it was cooked. But 'ow the 'ell can yer get a fire going, night like this."

"Just as well. Remember what 'appened last week, time we made a bit o' smoke."

"Mean when Bob was knocked out? Bit o' bad luck, that's all that was. Can't even do a bit o' cookin' now—it's come to that. Where's granddad?"

"Out with the officer, same as usual."

"More fool 'im—'e wasn't asked to go. Ought to know better, old soldier like 'im—'e ought to know."

"Always 'angin' round 'im, yer know 'e is. Watches 'im like a two-year-old. Gawd knows why."

"Wants it, p'raps." Dick Bartlett dug vigorously into the tin between his knees. "Bit of a kid, our officer. But he's growin' up. 'Ow's the kids, Beard?"

Beard warmed to the one subject that never failed to awaken interest.

"Ain't so bad. 'Ad a letter today. Bob's got a touch o' croup, and Lil she's teethin', but the missus says—'ere, where's the letter? I'll read yer what the missus says. Where the 'ell's that letter? 'Ere, get up, Bett, you're sittin' on my letter."

"Pity Brains ain't 'ere—'e'd make something of this bully beef." Bettson sat immovable, rolling a cigarette. "Gawd's sake, leave off shoving me about, yer blighter. 'Ow do I know where yer letter is? 'Tain't even as if it was good bully, because it ain't. Dish o' hot Maconochie now——"

"Or pork and beans—with the pork absorbed into the beans, same as what the good book says." Bartlett walked to the opening of the dug-out to watch the rain hissing past the sandbags into the black water at his feet.

"Bloody fools, them fellers that volunteered to go tonight. Don't suppose they'll get there. If they do they won't get back. Like 'ell tonight. 'Ullo, there's the star shells going up. That'll be them arriving. That's it—that's the machine guns opening from Bellewarde. Wonder who we'll get if Freddy Mann stops a packet."

"Brains, p'raps. 'E's takin' a commission soon. Sort o' feller that ought to. What are they makin' for?"

"Corner o' Bellewarde."

70

"An' there's Bavs there. Wurtemburgers. 'Ope they enjoys it, that's all I can say."

" 'Ere it is," said Beard. "This is what the missus says. Lil, she says, she's 'ad a rash, that comes o' teethin', the doctor says, and——"

"Now their bloody guns 'ave opened. That Wytschaete Willy, and there goes Percy over into Pop. Pleasant sort of a night this'll be before we're through. Who thought of this blasted raid?"

"Toler. Who d'yer think did—French or 'Aig?"

"Show on our own—that it?"

Dick Bartlett nodded. "Trust 'im for monkeying round and making trouble. Old Uncle was right in that. Remember what 'e used to say about winnin' the war. 'E was right about that. Too much nonsense Toler talks."

"Suppose we all talked it, same as a month ago. Damned green we was."

"Damned fools we was to come. Only thing to do now is to carry on quiet and get out quick. Mine's a left-arm Blighty."

"Might shove yer left 'and up above the trench, but they've made that court-martial now. Been a bloomin' wounded 'ero, with a left-hand Blighty last October. Ah well, we're a bit too late. Gawd, listen to the bloomin' raid."

The dug-out was silent for a minute.

"What's that?" asked Private Beard. "Their guns or lightnin'?"

"Both. There's the 'ell of a storm just overhead. And what with that, an' all these guns——"

"Wonder 'ow they're gettin' on? Old Uncle'll 'ave a tale to tell."

"Plenty 'e's got already—what with South Africa and India. Prize liars ain't in it with old Uncle. Damned old scoundrel, if ever there was one. But 'e looks after Freddy Mann proper. Say that for 'im, anyway."

" 'Ullo, Corporal, any news?"

A streaming head appeared at the dug-out entrance.

"Nope, except the German fleet's come out at Zillebeke."

"Raid, I mean."

"No. They're out there somewhere. Getting it 'ot, too. Back soon I suppose. Don't mean ter say Bett's guzzlin' still?"

"Thinks it's 'is duty. That's what Bett's 'ere to do, to guzzle. 'Ow many's out?"

"Seven. They'll probably stop a packet or two between them—damned fools to go—just because they've found a bomb or two. 'Ullo, what's up? There's something 'appening."

The others followed Corporal Garside along the flooded trench, towards where dark forms were moving quickly. The rain was white in the light of the star shells and Verey lights, and three separate streams of lead poured overhead.

"Keep down, yer bastards. They're comin' in. Somebody's bein' carried: thought as much. Wonder who it is. Anyway, 'tain't the officer, 'e's 'ere. Glad to see yer alive, sir. Thought as 'ow yer might 'ave stopped a packet. Anybody 'it, sir?"

"Yes, Brains. Got it through the leg. We just managed to get him in."

"Is he——?"

"He's a gonner, I'm afraid. Where are the stretcher bearers?"

"Look 'ere, Corporal." Private Bettson's voice was clear above the others in the confusion, as he lumbered up the trench. "What I want to know is, when the 'ell we're going to 'ave Maconochie instead o' bully beef?"

A lifeless form was carried down the trench, past an ex-docker turned soldier, who stood protesting, up to the knees in water, tin in hand.

CHAPTER XI

I⊤ is better in theory to be in company support than in the front line trench; better to be in battalion reserve somewhere by B.H.Q. than a hundred yards nearer the enemy; better to be in Brigade support at Ypres, than up at Railway Wood or Hooge; better than all to be in Brigade reserve and listen to the machine guns in the distance and watch the fireworks from Elverdinghe or Vlamertinghe. It is so in theory, but in practice it all depends. In the front line trench the majority of the rifle grenades, trench mortars and minnies available on the Western Front tend to be discharged at you, and you are sometimes struck by the resemblance between yourself and a target at the 200 yards range during musketry practice at Ash Ranges. Apart from that, unless an attack is imminent, the chances are that you may be left alone. If you are anywhere near B.H.Q. things tend to happen. Crumps of a heavier variety arrive, cheered by the company in the front line, who listen to them with glee as they sail over to disturb the R.Q.M. from his rations and his well-earned sleep. Also, you are nearer the Colonel, the Adjutant, and the trench-mortar dump, not altogether an unmixed advantage, and the Brigadier, when he visits the line, tends to ask why the devil you aren't out on trench fatigues instead of hanging about the dug-outs.

In Ypres these difficulties are accentuated, ammunition dumps being substituted for trench-mortar stores and the digging of cable trenches for trench fatigues. Furthermore, as Major Baggallay discovered, together with many both before and after, life in Ypres is a peculiar thing. Dug-outs and cellars that would be safe elsewhere are sometimes to be looked upon askance in Ypres. You shift your quarters, sometimes as the result of a hurried visit from a perturbed brigade major or staff captain, or of instinctive premonition, from north to south of the Menin Gate, or from a street near the Water Tower to the vicinity of the Prison, set your men in and settle down, your candle is suddenly extinguished or you are lifted bodily across your dug-out, and you wonder whether your reading of the riddle was correct. Finally, in brigade reserve at Vlamertinghe, these and other visitations come upon you thick and fast. There is at Vlamertinghe no lack of 8.6s and 5.9s, of brigade majors and inspecting generals, of days devoted to interior economy on an advanced scale, of rumours of imminent gas attacks and break-throughs by the Boche, of sudden orders detailing you to take a working party and report to an R.E. major or corporal at Birr Cross Roads at 10 p.m., and, if all else fails, there is always the Transport Officer to entertain when he "drops in to have one" on his way to the transport lines.

The news of the withdrawal for a week at Flammers was received with satisfaction and approval by "C" Company and the rest of the 8th Battalion of the Loyal Southshires. But within twenty-four hours Robbie and Freddy Mann, seated within a caisson, watching two farms going up in flames, pondering the unexplained deficiencies in kuives and mess tins and endeavouring to restore their tunics to some semblance of decency for the G.O.C.'s parade, realised what they were in for, and began to pine for the relative peace of Cambridge Road. There certainly wasn't much rest for subalterns at Vlamertinghe when Townroe, Toler, the M.O., the Quartermaster and the German shells were round about. They were there for six days, during which Freddy Mann had four inspections—one of a very special order to satisfy a Labour member who looked rather like a Belgian spy that we were winning the war—and spent the remainder of the time inquiring into the whereabouts of razors, socks and mess-tins, examining rifles, taking his platoon to divisional baths, receiving what Toler was pleased to call map instruction, doing his battalion and platoon parades and taking working parties for routine jobs behind the line. But it was a merry enough time, with reasonable weather and flea-bags to sleep in at night, and the Fancies at "Pop" in the evening when he wasn't booked. With the shelling, too, they were lucky on the whole. They got on to the transport lines once or twice, but that did the Q.M. good, and as far as actual casualties, they only dropped six from "C" Company and none from his platoon. And, after all, if they were to return to the line on Thursday, there was Wednesday ahead; and on Wednesday Toler, with a sudden access of humanity or as a result of Harry's persuasion, had told Robbie and himself that they could shove off for a day's lorry jumping and get back when they liked, and—the message was conveyed through Harry—they didn't want to see their ugly faces till they turned up on parade next morning.

•   •   •   •   •

"Eight weeks today," remarked Freddy Mann, as he set his glass upon the table and leaned back in the corner of the little Watou estaminet.

"Eight ruddy weeks," corroborated Derek Robinson. He blew into the bowl of his pipe with even more than his usual slow deliberation. "Eight ruddy weeks. What about another drink?"

"Yes. Remember passing here, eight weeks ago. Seems longer. Seems the hell of a time since then. Rather thrilled we were at the idea of going up to Wipers. Not much thrill about it now. Remember that old dame at Watten? She knew all about it. Since May we've been there—devil of a time since May. Why don't they put the 9th in and take us out a bit? Getting fed up with it, the men."

"Don't blame 'em. Hullo, who's this?" as the door swung open and a conspicuously martial figure appeared.

"Morning. Morning all!" The newcomer was obviously of a markedly friendly disposition. "Mind if I join you? Damned hot today. Phew! Cognac, mademoiselle. Sure,"— as if with an afterthought—"I'm not butting in? Kaye of the A.S.C. I am. Quite sure I'm not butting in? Glad to see you, you know. Don't often see people in this damned place. Get out of it when I can. Rotten job, the A.S.C. Rotten place,

Belgium—dull, damned dull—that's what's the matter here. Have another with me. Don't you find it dull?"

"Well." Robinson refilled his pipe. "We've come up from Ypres, you see. In brigade reserve and we got a day off. You wouldn't call it dull there—no, dull's not exactly quite the word."

"Ypres. Ah yes, I know Ypres." Lieutenant Kaye nodded with infinite wisdom. "Know Ypres well. Seen it more than once, matter o' fact. Seen it from Vlamertinghe, Brielen, places round like that. So you find it a bit on the lively side, up there at Ypres?"

"Tends to be, you know."

"Ah well." Lieutenant Kaye looked with a cheerful and reassuring smile upon the rather pale curly-haired subaltern on his left and the raw-boned Devonian in front of him. "Make the best of it, as I do—that's what you'll have to do. Devil of a long time yet we'll be there."

"You think so? Is that the feeling here?"

"That's what they all say, all those that know. I was up at 2nd Army yesterday, and met a fellow there who's in the know, one of the high-up Johnnies, don't you know. He was telling me all about it. They don't worry, any of 'em. Just a matter of time it is, that's all. But it's bound to take some time."

"What?"

"Wearing 'em out—you know our game. Killing each other off, you know, and see who can keep it up for the longest. That's our game."

"Is it?"

"Yes. Bound to be. Pays us, because we're bound to win. Fellow I saw at Cassel, he worked it out. Got it here somewhere I believe—yes, here it is."

Lieutenant Kaye produced from the pocket of his immaculate and well-cut tunic a folded paper covered on both sides with scribbled figures.

"Yes, this is it. We were working it out after dinner. This is how he reckons it. Say the Germans have 3,000,000 effectives and we can put 6,000,000 into the field altogether, and the casualties on each side on all fronts are roughly 100,000 a month—70 per cent. of those wounded, allow 30 per cent. of those return—let's see, how did he work it out?"

Freddy Mann and Robbie glanced at each other and remained silent while the prophecies of the unknown priest of Delphi were disentangled and expounded. Lieutenant Kaye thought a moment, scribbled a few additional figures hastily and then looked up with a cheery smile.

"That's it, that's got it. Allow a million and a half to keep the front, let each side drop 1,200,000 a year, of which 800,000 return, put on 300,000 each year for those going up, take off 100,000 for general wastage and that's—no, it isn't—anyway, I remember he worked it out to something between four years and five. Didn't think much would happen before then."

"And what happens then?"

"German front collapses and in we go. Perfectly simple; it can't go wrong. It's just a matter of time, and not getting hurried, that's all it is. He explained it all to me—clever chap—fellow on the Staff, you know. They get all this worked out there. Nothing left to chance at G.H.Q." He nodded solemnly, ordered another cognac and looked inquiringly at the others.

"You hadn't looked at it quite like that before?"

"Well." The Cherub looked half amused and half perplexed. Robbie solemnly shook his head, and filled his pipe.

"No?"

"Ah well, glad I told you. Cheer you up; it's bound to, to know how it's working out. But that's why I say, you'll have a good deal more of Wipers."

"What about you?"

"Don't worry me. Nice fat job, this job, car o' me own whenever I want it, decent pay, spot o' leave this summer— all the same to me. Let the war go on for all I care and the more of it the better. Haven't got any job to go back to—just hanging about at home. Same with this fellow I was telling you about—it doesn't worry him. Six hundred thousand he reckoned our total casualties this year—bound to take some time. Not keeping you chaps, am I?"

"No. We're just out for the day, no special programme."

"How are you getting round?"

"Lorry jumping. Came up by Proven, and we're going back through Pop."

"Pop. I thought of running in there meself. Got a little bit in 5 Bis, you know," with a knowing grin. "Tell you what. Come and have a spot of lunch with me, and

we'll flip down to Pop this evening and dine and see the
Fancies. You can easily shove along from there at any
time. That's what we'll do—you just come along. Just
along there's our mess—just along the road. Just one
more and then we'll push along."

·   ·   ·   ·   ·

Given the company and the freedom, there was nothing
better than a day in Pop. What Blackpool is to Lancashire,
or Brighton to the Metropolis, that, or something like it,
was Poperinghe to the Salient in 1915. The members of the
A.S.C. mess appeared as care-free as Lieutenant Kaye, and
two of his fellows found after a cheerful lunch that it was
possible for them to tear themselves away from their duties
and accompany them on the flivver down the road from
Watou, through St. Jan-ter-Biezen. In Pop itself they had
tea, indulged in a little desultory shopping, dined, arranged
to meet Lieutenant Kaye outside 5 Bis, within the hallowed
portals of which it was not apparently thought advisable that
they should enter, and to finish the evening dropped in at
the Fancies, where Freddy Mann, thoughts of raids, stand-
tos and shelling far removed, helped to cheer Margarine and
Glycerine to the echo and joined manfully in the chorus
of Jerry Brum. Good sort of a day, they concluded, as they
finally bade goodnight outside the Town Hall and Robbie
and he set out past the station on their homeward trek. A
peaceful day, fine weather, and a peaceful night. There was
nothing the matter with the Wipers Road on a night like

this. Just the usual traffic moving along—ambulances, a few guns, an odd working party or two, a battalion of the neighbouring division moving from the line—nothing ahead but the usual star shells and clatter of machine guns, and just a little shelling here and there. Somewhere in the region of Vlamertinghe it seemed to be, but as something usually was happening in that region of Vlamertinghe, there was nothing much in that.

"P'raps it's Goldfish Château," remarked Robbie hopefully. "About time they had something at D.H.Q. Let's shove along. It'll probably die down soon."

After a few minutes even this disturbance ceased, and the subalterns walked for the last mile along a quiet and deserted road to turn the somewhat forbidding corner by the mill and take the lane to the left that led towards their huts. Here for the first time they were conscious of some disturbance: figures were moving quickly in the distance, and two men, one an officer, were doubling down the lane.

"What's the matter with Harry?" asked Freddy Mann, as the tense features appeared in the darkness, lips drawn thin and white and the corners of the mouth hard set. "What's up, Harry? Anything up?"

"Go and see. They got on to us, the devils. Six direct hits. Done Malcolm in and knocked out B.G. and God knows how many in "C" Company alone. Better get along and help. 'Bout time you came. Better get along and see what they've left of your platoons. Where the hell are those ambulances? Sort of thing that would happen. You get along."

There was nothing to the already partially trained eyes of Freddy Mann and Robbie unusual in the sight they saw by the wrecked huts one hundred yards to the left of the lane. They'd seen men bleeding to death before, an officer minus a leg, a head lying by itself in the corner of a field, figures tossing on stretchers and moaning as they rolled along the ground. It was a little unexpected, perhaps, and it seemed a curious thing to return from a peaceful countryside, peasants working in fields and children playing on the roads, to this. But, as Freddy Mann realised as he knelt to close Malcolm's eyes, it showed that it was difficult to know what would happen next at Ypres, and that the theory of the war of attrition so well expounded by Kaye was working as it should. This loss of eighty men meant 120 casualties in the last ten days of rest. Roughly, that tallied with the figures, and so long as the number was not exceeded we might expect to win the war.

CHAPTER XII

Der Colonel Ludwig von Rutter stood still as any statue upon the firestep, listening to the stream of shells that screamed towards the west, and peering through the darkness towards the bursts of fire upon the trenches three hundred yards away. There was a certain tension in his manner; for some days he had spoken even less, and delivered his orders in an even sharper voice than usual. This was to some extent to be attributed to the strain of trench warfare. Colonel von Rutter was doubtless beginning to feel the need for leave: since October he had been at this game, since October he had promised from time to time first his company and then his battalion that they should be in Ypres within three days and at the sea within a week. Far be it from Colonel von Rutter to say that the men were ceasing to believe it; but the fact remained that things were not going quite the way they should. These offensives had a habit of succeeding up to a point, but never quite coming off. October 31st—they ought to have been through that day: he had been told as a fact since that there had been nothing at all behind the British line except headquarters, and they had had division after division coming up, the roads behind packed with troops and guns from Menin back to Courtrai. Then again, last April, Pilckem, St. Julien, Frezenberg, Hooge—they were all but through; he had seen the towers of Ypres from the woods beyond the château, had looked on the railway crossing from a distance of only three fields away; but always at the last moment some straggling disordered lines would come toiling up the slopes, or struggling through the shell-fire of the Menin Road, pressing on and on as if every inch of those few square miles of ground was of greater value than their very souls. And now, to crown all, that last attack in June, when they had actually been turned out of the Hooge Château by a crowd of wild, yelling barbarians dressed in women's skirts. Von Hügel himself had been pretty fed up about that, and he wasn't the only one. When it comes to Duke Albrecht himself sending Ilse, his chief-of-staff, up to Gheluvelt to ask what the devil they were playing at.—No—Colonel von Rutter stiffened his back and pressed his lips together—it wasn't good enough. The men's discipline was all right still, but they were getting a bit sick of it, beginning to talk a bit among themselves; and it wasn't the men only, or even his own reputation or that of his battalion: there was something more in it than that. This Ypres, that was really nothing more than a Belgian market town, was beginning to be talked of by the British apparently as a symbol, almost as a holy place, a sort of Belgian Verdun. Well, if that were so, the issues must be joined: if they had staked their strength in its defence, it was the German might, the German God against the British in the last resort. "Gott strafe . . ." Yes, and sooner or later he would do it here. Von Rutter looked a moment from the dank grass and wire to the quiet stars above. There—there—somewhere in the universe of distance, riding the storm of battle, was the God of their Fathers, whose hand was with them still. If till now He had denied them victory, it was but that victory might be the sweeter when it came and men better for chastening might reap it. They had striven before to win their way down the last two miles of that tortured road and failed; but tonight they would fight through, even if it were through Hell to the gates of Paradise: hell—nay, rather hell should be their ally, for the fires of hell should help them. Poison is good, but a man may choke and live; but can a man live when the cloud that comes upon him is a cloud of fire? One last look upward and out to where the shells burst unceasingly, and von Rutter moved to join another figure which was busying itself beneath the parapet of the next fire bay. The younger officer, as his Colonel approached, turned, straightened himself and gave a stiff salute.

"All well, Karl?"

"All well, Herr Colonel."

"It is ready?"

"Yes."

The officers looked at each other with understanding eyes.

"This time, I think."

"Yes, I believe this time: nothing can stand against it."

"So we thought about our gas: but still—this time."

He leaned his arms upon the parapet facing eastward.

"Hell there." He pointed to the bursts. "That is hell—for them. There goes a body now." He pointed to a dark object that circled for a moment in the air. "And for ten days they have had it: there can be little left."

"They have put fresh troops in there tonight. Kurt told me at Brigade."

Von Rutter nodded.

"I know. New troops—those of Kitchener."

He smiled.

"The better for us, good Karl. Old men, boys from school, clerks, keepers of shops, and for them—this." He pointed to the bottom of the trench, then stood for a moment silent.

"It is ten to three. But thirty minutes more. The men are ready?"

"Yes."

"Your company shall win the honour, Karl. It is time— that God was with us. This time—tomorrow is the last day of July. By August we shall be there." A sudden new light appeared two miles away. "That is Ypres burning. They are the flames of wrath. It is the funeral pyre. By sword and flame, good Karl. Our sword tonight shall be a sword of fire."

•   •   •   •   •

That was Robbie. Well, anyway, thank God he was still alive. So long as Robbie was still alive there would be someone on his left, between him and the Menin Road.

That was the thing to remember tonight, that the Menin Road was on his left: it had always been on his right before, with Y Wood in between them. Y Wood was across there now, and these woods here were Zouave and Sanctuary Wood, that he had never been near before. He must keep that clear, whatever happened: and this was their support line and whatever happened they mustn't budge, not even if the companies in front, up at Hooge there, couldn't stick it. The other fellows they relieved had stuck it for ten days on end, but perhaps it hadn't been quite as bad as this. He didn't see how many people could be left alive at Hooge— even in "C" Company there'd been three people blown to bits since they got in three hours ago, and God knows how many wounded. Yes, that was Robbie. He thought that shell had got him, but there he was. Funny how cool he kept, but he was always cool like that. Perhaps it was easy to keep cool if you didn't get that feeling in your legs and knees: his own would hardly work now, when it came to climbing over sandbags. Still, he'd just get round this traverse and meet Robbie at the sentry post. There was something moving there, so Gibbs was still alive as well. They'd burst in the sap-head, which was a pity, but if they went on shelling like this they couldn't help bursting in everything in time, which he hoped wouldn't happen, as it would take a long time to build it all again and——

"Cheer-oh!"

How the devil did he manage to keep his voice so natural in this filthy row? He was just exactly the same as if he was at Aldershot.

"Just came along to see if all was O.K. here. You all right?"

He was talking a bit more slowly. Well, of course, he would. But that was all.

"Yes. We're all right."

"Lost many?"

"Three for certain. None in the last half-hour."

Robbie nodded and paused, looking up the hill to Hooge.

"Pretty thick up—up there: it's worse than here. They've got machine guns from Hooge as well. It looks as if they're coming."

Freddy Mann tried to lick his lips, but his tongue was sticky. He made a praiseworthy attempt to swallow some moisture that wasn't there.

"About as nasty a night as any that we've had."

Freddy Mann swallowed again.

"Do you think—anything is up?"

"Dunno. Toler thinks there may be. And Harry's in a filthy temper—that's usually a sign of something."

"Wonder why they shoved us in the line?"

"Give the other chaps a rest probably. Ten days of it they've had on end. Up to us, I suppose, to take the bowling. They're getting it pretty bad up there. Getting in must have been the devil of a job on a night like this. Well." He glanced round and back at Freddy Mann. "Suppose I'd better get along and see about our rations. Think I'll go back this way," as he clambered up into No Man's Land. "Just see if all's O.K. along the wire. Biggs seems happy enough." He nodded towards the figure in the tumbled sap-head. "So long. I'll be just along here—if anything should happen: it's a sticky sort of night."

Robbie nodded casually and passed along towards the road. With him there seemed to Freddy Mann to vanish one of the few hopes of sanity that remained. Robbie seemed to take all this as natural. He was older, of course; perhaps that made the difference. For himself he'd have to stick it out, but it wasn't easy, as his head was dancing a bit, and he kept on shivering and feeling funny whenever a shell came near. What was the use of calling this "standing up to bowling"? You could stand up to bowling all right, when you had a chance, but out here, if you weren't shot through the head like Ark-wright, you were blown to bits like Ford and Graveson were last week, and all the time there were those poor swine of Tommies depending on you, so you couldn't say what you felt, and all these corpses and blood and things about, just because the Staff said they had to stick it out in front of Ypres, which everybody knew was a damned silly thing to do, with these crumps pouring down and the earth rocking—and now what the hell was up? He leaned forward over the parapet as some new devilry broke out at Hooge, accompanied by redoubled machine-gun fire, flicker and fall of starlights, and between them arches of fire that seemed to rise into the heavens and fall in lines of sparks to earth just where the front line companies must be.

"What the hell——"

"Steady, lad, now steady. Are you ready here?"

Freddy Mann turned to face his Company Commander.

"Is it an attack?"

"Think so. It'll be all right, lad. Just keep steady. Yes, there's the S.O.S. and that's our guns: just stick it. Keep 'em steady. All right?"

"Yes—but what the devil's that?"

"Dunno—damned if I know, to tell you the truth. Might be anything—new star shells or something. Been watching it for the last few minutes, matter o' fact. It's——"

He looked again, a little puzzled. He was a conscientious, rather fussy Regular soldier, well versed in his job and in military history; but his mentality, and, as it proved, his knowledge of human nature had its limits: he could not know that at that moment men were screaming, cutting their throats with bayonets and blowing their brains out, while their flesh was being gnawed and stripped from their bones by liquid fire.

●　　●　　●　　●　　●

Why didn't Corporal Sugger get up? What was the use of lying squealing at the bottom of a trench? Hadn't he often said that the one thing he wanted to do was to see a Hun? Hadn't he often told 'em all about exactly what he was going to do with 'em when he met 'em? This was his chance. He wouldn't have a better chance than this. Didn't he want to see them? There they were to see, coming on like grey ants, shoving along past their left towards Zouave Wood, dozens of 'em, hundreds—ants growing bigger all over the ground with some khaki chaps being

driven along in front of them. They weren't advancing in
very good order, but they were coming nearer. Somehow
they'd got to stop them. Whatever happened they mustn't
get into the trenches, Townroe said. But the shelling didn't
seem to stop them, or the machine guns: the more that
fell the more it seemed came on over the crest by Hooge.
The companies there hadn't stopped them: they were
getting round behind them now. He could even hear the
men cheering and shouting between the bursts of shell
fire: first time he'd seen them in all these weeks, first time
almost it really seemed to him that they were real. Why
couldn't they stop and give them just a moment—only
fair, after all that shelling, to give them just a breathing
space. But you couldn't expect much from chaps who'd
go and pour fire over people, like that fellow from Hooge
said they'd done up there. This was the end, perhaps. Bit
too fast, this bowling. They'd got to be stopped, Townroe
said, and they kept on coming on, so—hullo he was
coming for him, that fellow, making a bee-line straight at
him through the wire. Well, here's for the revolver. Might
get him. He hadn't practised much with his revolver, but
it was the only chance—oh, damned good shot, that.
That was Bamford. Always a good chap, Bamford. They
seemed to be stopping a bit now at last. Didn't blame 'em,
with so many hanging on the wire, and others lying on
their backs and squirming about all over the place and
crawling through the grass. There were no more coming,
either, now. Our machine guns—that's what it was, those
M.M.G. fellows and Robbie's Lewis gun. Oh, damned

good if they'd stopped them. Bit of a mess they'd made though. Look at this one fire-bay, or what used to be a fire-bay, and Beale and Holter sprawling dead across the parapet, and Price bleeding to death in that corner, and Howell groping about as if he couldn't see—just Bamford and himself left, and Sugger squealing and lying on his face. He'd be shot for cowardice most likely. Here was Harry coming. He'd fix him. Damned fool he was to carry on like that. You didn't stop the Hun by lying at the bottom of a trench, shrieking and calling out for God. Fool he'd look, when he got up again and he found that while he'd been lying there they'd stopped the Hun. Yes, here come the shells again. They wouldn't be shelling those trenches if they hadn't known the attack had failed. Good bit of work, that, to have stopped the Hun. Never mind the shelling. They'd stopped——

. . . . .

An hour to go. Glad he'd got back from the dressing station in time after that crack on the head in the trench yesterday morning. Hadn't known much about yesterday, and what he had was apparently all wrong. It wasn't at them at all that they were going, but at those fellows on the left. They'd had a pretty thin time, his crowd, up in the air all day and fired at from front and side and rear. One way of sleeping through it, anyway, to get knocked out by a bit of shell and be for six hours unconscious in a dug-out. Getting back to Sanctuary Wood last night was about the first thing he remembered. Now they were there, why the devil did they leave it? Damned silly idea, attacking Hooge by daylight. Putting the whole Brigade in, were they? Jolly few there'd be left this time tomorrow. Silly to leave a place like this. Not much to look at, with half the trees down and shells crashing into it every few minutes, but it was better than the open; they could move about here, and a fly couldn't move out there without being pipped. No dog's chance of getting across the open this afternoon, any more than those other poor swine had of getting across the Menin Road upon their left. Harry had practically said so, and it was easy to guess what Townroe thought. Chucking away men like this, good chaps all of them, fellows he'd got to know well, fellows like Beale and Price and Holter. Hadn't got Robbie, though, or Bamford—glad of that, as he glanced at Bamford, looming heavily by his side and putting a stray bullet away in his pouch. One hour—he was still feeling sick and dizzy, and suddenly Bamford's figure seemed to dance and disappear, and in place of it the bullet grew ever larger and larger, till at last it filled the trench before him, a gigantic dark pointed mass spread across the scarred earth and trees, with a number which he could not quite decipher in blood and figures round the base. He felt for his "cold mutton ticket"—second Lieutenant Frederick Drydale Mann, No. 45231. Good luck to it! One hour to go.

·   ·   ·   ·   ·

If only they could see the bottom of that tree. Two hundred yards more, and they could get to the crest and see it. If it was possible, they'd do it, but it was just as Bamford had said, just like Magersfontein over again. Shove on, though. Robbie was shoving on, and there was Townroe and Toler out in front, and Bill's crowd on his right. Shove on; it didn't matter about the other bullets, didn't particularly matter now even if that one came along—getting there was all that mattered. But they couldn't do it. Just about here was where the first wave had stuck. Nearby those leading platoons lay all in rows. Here was Hooker, a shell seemed to have got him pretty badly. Let's see if they could get a little further— just a yard further, just for the sake of doing it. Get up, Johnson. If you must fall, don't fall on your bayonet. Oh you can't get up; that's one less. How's that on Kaye's theory? All right, but it's the getting on that's difficult. Nobody seems to be getting any further now. Townroe's stopped, they've all stopped. Perhaps they'll go on when the Hun has fired all his ammunition. But there won't be many left. Nice job for Scribner, making out the casualty lists tonight. Back, is it? Withdraw, not retire, don't forget that—no such order as retire today. Withdraw sounds better—but retire or withdraw, they've got to go back the way they came. Bloody fool, the Corps Commander. Pity he wasn't here to enjoy it all himself. Get back—they'd damned well take Hooker and Johnson with them. Shove Johnson on your back, Bamford; I'll look after Hooker. Tell Bettson to fix up Biggs—no chance for him, if he's left out here: give me his rifle. We'll get back somehow, many as we can, to Sanctuary Wood. Can't miss the way. There's bodies all the way back to show us. Wonder if there's any rum left in Sanctuary Wood. Not the way it worked out last year by Cæsar's Camp or on Laffan's Plain. Things don't often go as they should in front of Ypres. All right, Bamford, you can put him down now; we're back in Sanctuary Wood. He's dead, is he? Perhaps he was dead when we picked him up. But we'll stop the rats or Huns from getting him tonight.

· · · · ·

"Beat up the band, for God's sake." They were ready now, all fallen in. There wouldn't be any more, however long they waited. No use counting them over again. Thirty-two made thirty-two and why shouldn't a company have thirty-two? "A" Company only had six, and "B" Company ten, so why worry if "C" Company had thirty-two. He'd done well, had Freddy Mann; he'd brought fourteen out alive. No more to come—get on. Robbie was here and Toler and Bill and Harry—they were all ready except the band. There were plenty, too, to make a band. Give Baines a drum, and bugles to Hall and Grimes, they could blow bugles and Grimes could hobble along somehow, because it had missed his knee. Townroe was here now, and Toler on his horse, riding up and down beside them, riding damned badly, and blocking half the traffic outside the Goldfish Château.

Never mind that, the traffic would have to look after itself for once. There was the G.O.C. watching, and half the Staff, and here were some fellows of the 1st who'd strolled across from Dickebusch to see them. They were all ready, and they could form fours just as well with thirty-two men as with 200. Might have given them buses, perhaps, to get them back, but as they hadn't it didn't matter; back on their own they'd go, the band was all they wanted. Buck up the band. Shove in Fyles, if you want another bugle—double up, Fyles, they want you for a bugle, and you've got as much breath left as anybody, put your head up, that's the way. That's it now, drumsticks crossed, bugles ready, Townroe up in front and Robbie just behind him with three rows of fours between. Now for it—"Tipperary," that's the tune—just what they want, this, to help them keep the step. Oh, keep step, for God's sake, Bettson. You've stopped the Hun and you're going back to rest. I know you're pretty well all in, but keep step, old son, same as the rest of us. Let's all keep step— that's it, heads up. Sing—damned crowd of scarecrows, and we didn't do all we wanted, but we're off back now to St. Jan-ter-Biezen and we've stopped the Hun.

CHAPTER XIII

CAPTAIN FREDDY DALE sipped his whisky and regarded rather fixedly the officer who faced him, toying with pencil and paper and looking at him with indifferent gaze. If it were possible to credit such a thing of so finished a production of Camberley, it would almost have appeared as if Captain Dale were nervous at the prospect of the forthcoming interview. The situation was admittedly difficult, especially as Captain Dale, in addition to his determination to fulfil his duties as Corps representative, was conscious of the obligation laid upon him as a human being to give some inkling of the feeling that existed up at Proven. It would hardly be fair to let this Colonel, who seemed a sufficiently good fellow, go blundering on to his fate in the fond belief that all was well, when as a matter of fact, in the eyes of the Corps Commander, all was very far from well. So far, Colonel Townroe had remained regrettably unresponsive to his openings. He would lift up his head a little, look at him rather vaguely, pass the whisky or the cigarettes over and wait for him to speak. Well, as things were, let the human touch come afterwards: he couldn't well go wrong if he stuck to the mission on which he had been sent.

"It is just, you understand, Colonel, that the Corps Commander wishes to get a clear picture in his mind of what was happening: and you were on the spot. Can you tell me exactly what was happening, say at four o'clock that afternoon, before—er—the order came to withdraw to Sanctuary Wood?"

"We were being potted at—that's about all there is to it."

"And about 6 p.m. the order came to withdraw?"

"Yes."

"From Brigade?"

"From Brigade or the War Office. It came, anyway. Have a drink?"

"Thanks. Well——" Freddy Dale's note book was in his hand. "Was it in your opinion—strictly necessary?"

Colonel Townroe raised his eyebrows.

"May I put it this way—if you had been in sole command, without any possibility of receiving orders—I put the case quite hypothetically—would you have—er—withdrawn?"

Colonel Townroe's eyes narrowed a trifle. He made no reply.

"You see——" Freddy Dale struck a match and held it a moment before lighting a cigarette. "The Corps Commander feels——"

"The Corps Commander wasn't there."

"The Corps Commander feels," he repeated with some decision, "that it might have been possible——" He stopped.

"Well, go on. What does the Corps Commander feel?"

The Corps Commander's feelings were, it appeared, definite and explicit. The Corps Commander had made a careful study of the situation from the beginning, from the launching of the attack. He had scrutinised personally all reports and orders that had come into his hands, and had questioned at some length some twenty-seven eye-witnesses, including three prisoners who had been brought to Proven that morning. He had, of course, taken the G.O.C. and brigadiers concerned into the fullest consultation before coming to his decision, but his decision, although he, Captain Dale, regretted to have to announce it, was that——"

"We ratted?"

Freddy Dale waved a deprecatory hand. No such thought he was sure was consciously in the minds of any of them, but in view of all the circumstances, it would appear that perhaps the position, both at Hooge and before Sanctuary Wood, was abandoned with undue haste, and without due regard——

"That's all very well, but what about our casualties? Do you know what we are losing?"

Freddy Dale was now on firmer ground. The Corps Commander was of opinion, with which he was sure that all would agree, that there were occasions upon which less regard must be paid to casualties than normally was the case. There were crises in trench warfare, as in all forms of warfare, in which prime regard must be paid, not to the toll of human life that was being exacted, but to the requirements of the situation, the morale of the remaining troops, the honour of the regiment.

"This affair," Captain Dale continued in more confident tones, "has left an unfortunate impression. I tell you this, you understand, as between ourselves. It does not fall within my official duties." He paused before he continued.

"Yes, yes. Go on."

"Very well, then, if I may speak openly, it has tended to create the impression at Corps and elsewhere that the value of Kitchener's Army as a fighting unit has been exaggerated. It is the first affair of any consequence in which a division of the New Army has been engaged. Notice has necessarily been taken of it, reports have been called for from G.H.Q. and from the War Office, and it stands to reason that the nature of those reports——"

"Have another drink."

"Not now. It is understood, of course, that the Brigade and you yourself were placed in a difficult situation: full allowances have been made for the unexpectedness of the attack, the rawness of the troops, the strangeness of the ground. But the Corps Commander—we at Proven were not quite sure if you personally fully appreciated the situation. Your reports are non-committal and appear to show no realisation of failure. While although this is perhaps in itself a minor matter, the marching back of the troops to the accompaniment of a band—you know, Colonel"—with a sudden access of humanity—"I hate all this."

"That's all right. Help yourself."

"I'm damned sorry in myself for you."

"That's all right."

"Bad luck—we all know it's damned bad luck. It's only what the Corps Commander feels. He's fed up. That's why he's putting in the other crowd to get the trenches back. It's only that I had to tell you."

"That's all right. Don't worry." The Colonel sat immovable and imperturbable as ever.

"I hope it won't have harmed your fellows, don't you know."

"It's difficult to harm the dead."

CHAPTER XIV

H E was one of the best of the War Correspondents upon the Western Front. Nine months of war experience, combined with his professional knowledge and training, enabled him to separate the essential from the unessential and to give to the British public just that information which it required upon the things that mattered, such as the nature of the struggle, the magnitude of the issues involved, and the morale of the troops. He did not believe in writing up from theory or hearsay, but preferred to portray events and characters as he saw them with his own eyes in the course of his regulated wanderings. It was at places like this that he would, he had discovered, obtain the material that he wanted. At G.H.Q. and behind the Corps area the war tended to become rather remote, but here at St. Jan-ter-Biezen, in Corps reserve, he could find those who practically until yesterday had been engaged in hand-to-hand conflict, and who now had leisure to recount something of their experiences in that forbidden land which even he was not allowed to enter. He would see for himself of what manner of stuff the battalion of "K.1" was made. He had heard stories on the way up, some not altogether favourable. Never mind stories. He was not

Bowles of the *Daily Thunderer*, who spent his time in the messes and the hospitals at the Base: he would get among them, and form judgment for himself.

The day at St. Jan-ter-Biezen proved to be a day well spent. He was glad to see at the outset that the appalling losses which they had suffered had not quelled the military instincts of the battalion. They paraded as usual for battalion drill, and he noticed that the peculiar variations of detail in arms drill and formal manœuvre upon which the Southshires had prided themselves from time immemorial were observed as punctiliously by these soldiers of less than a year's standing as they could possibly have been by the 1st Battalion itself at Aldershot. He availed himself of the ample opportunities which Chip Viner, the Adjutant, afforded him of inspecting the huts and mess-rooms, and found, as he expected to find, that they were scrupulously orderly and clean. At B.H.Q. itself everybody, from the Colonel downwards, was busily occupied, and he noticed that both here and in the Quartermaster's department much time was being spent upon the composition of casualty lists and the sorting of effects. It was a sad business, but it was being executed in a thorough unemotional manner which spoke volumes for the spirit of those remaining.

In the afternoon, after a lunch at Headquarters mess, at which conversation seemed hardly less free than usual, and in which the Colonel seemed to have been in particularly good form, he walked across to the adjacent field to watch the games which Harry, the old Carlisle three-quarter, and Robbie had organised. They were playing both Soccer and Rugger with a will, officers and men together, keen as mustard for "C" Company to beat the rest. Best of good signs, this, and the note-book was plied that afternoon. Nothing much the matter with the spirit of an Army in which men could come straight from Ypres to a game of football. That was the sort of thing that people at home might take a lesson from: no grousing or repining here, but on with the game with a swing, and jolly good luck to the next attack. Then, after tea, when the parades and inspections of the day were over, what of those little groups jesting round by their tents, ambling about or playing the eternal House—"Click, click," "Top of the 'ouse"—happy to all appearance, happy and care-free, forgetting already their grim experiences. What men they were! And how the heart of the British public should swell with pride when it read any portrayal, however inadequate, of their daily life.

And if this could be said of the men, what could be said to do justice to the officers? If they had had to combine four messes into one, if out of the full complement but the C.O., acting Adjutant, two company commanders and five subalterns were remaining, then those remaining would see to it that in that one joint mess the old traditions should be maintained, and that the spirit of the British officer and gentleman should prevail over all adversity. They'd been through it all right; he could see that with half an eye. He wasn't like that fool Derry, of the *Wire*, who always pretended that the British soldier was insensible to suffering. He saw the marks of strain. Toler, heavy-eyed and chalky in appearance, looked as if he hadn't slept for days. Bill's hands were trembling, and he guessed that that was not from excessive smoking. That Devonian's tunic seemed a bit too loose round the neck, and that little curly-haired, quiet-voiced chap in the corner, whom they called Cherub and Ganymede when the port came round—his eyes were skeery, and he was pretty well all in: he couldn't speak without a slight stammer, and his head kept twitching. Yes, by God, they were men to bite on the bullet and keep it up like this. He could picture those others, to whom they would refer from time to time as the talk went eternally from the latest show in Town or the chances of conscription coming to Hooge and Sanctuary Wood. He could picture Roffey standing on top of his parapet at Hooge, to fall with a dozen dead Germans round him headlong on his wire; Wray walking out towards the advancing enemy to pick up a soldier whom he had noticed lying wounded in a shell-hole as they were falling back; B.G. the tough tea-planter, standing at a sap-head, still firing steadily with his clothes on fire. Lies, lies all the way, had been told of this division. Those at the Corps who'd downed them so were liars, and he'd see they knew it. He'd got the story clear enough, and they'd hung on where it was hardly possible for men to remain and live: and it was through these men, and those they led, that Sanctuary Wood and Ypres were ours. Their comrades had died at their posts, or had their lives sacrificed uselessly in that counter-attack, supreme act of a general's folly. But these remained, and with them lived something more—the spirit of a regiment that death itself could not overcome.

It was a fruitful visit. He was thanked by many for his article "The Spirit that Prevails," an article which went far to steady public opinion at a critical time. He narrated nothing that he did not see, he exaggerated nothing, he put nothing into the mouth of officer or man that had not actually been said in his presence. He paid no more than the tribute that was due. He did not tell, because he did not know, of the company commander who, with ten men left of those 200 whom he had tried to guard and train, fingered his revolver late that night, put it apparently idly to his temple, then suddenly flung it with a curse out into the darkness, or of that other, the Colonel, who wrote in his war diary "Ichabod," and walked the lanes all night alone.

CHAPTER XV

FREDDY MANN put back his final stake into his pocket, gathered up the kitty and a 50-franc note from the grunting and admiring Harry, helped himself to a final not illiberal whisky and soda, and with a cheery "Evening all. Three o'clock—must be pushing along. Thanks for a damned good evening," swung out of the farm-house to his billet. He whistled as he made his way across the field, lit his candle and slowly undressed in front of his shack, then lit a cigarette and took a final stroll, clad in pyjamas and British warm, to the corner of the enclosure before turning in. A very reasonable ending to a very reasonable sort of day. Nothing like doing Harry down at poker to finish with, especially when Harry threw in a full house and he held a pair of nines. There wasn't much in doing down those two kids who'd joined "C" Company since he left: they were sitting birds, those kids Ball and Trench, who'd just come from England with the latest draft, jumped whenever they heard a shell, and couldn't tell a joker from an ace of spades.

But Harry was a different matter. He'd given him his first lessons in poker a bare six months ago; he wondered how much he imagined he could teach him now? Yes, and what applied to poker applied to dozens of other things as well in this ruddy war. Damned fine soldier, Harry, one of the best he'd ever seen, and he would make something of the new "C" Company now that the Skipper had gone to Intelligence, if anybody could. He'd taught him more by example than by talk, most of the tricks of the trade. But was there now much more that he had to learn? He didn't want to buck, but there it was. Townroe had thought him good enough to give him the Battalion bombers, and from what he'd heard so far he hadn't exactly cramped their style. There might be something in that hint Chips had dropped of a "mention" for that July business for all he knew, and, anyway, there was no getting round the fact that the second pip had come through that morning. He'd had four months of it, and seen a bit, but no, he cheerfully reassured himself as he plunged into the darkness of his little triangular abode, the Huns had done their damnedest with him and he was still top-dog. That little singing in his head was nothing. They'd find before they finished that he was by no means done for yet; as Robbie would say, so far he'd played the bowling. And yes, by God, he'd learnt a bit since April.

He had. Take a boy of nineteen from school, put him into uniform, send him abroad, and give him within the space of nine months fifty-six days in the trenches by the Menin Road, and thirty days and nights in Ypres, and he will tend to grow in what passes in a war for wisdom. There wasn't much that Freddy Mann hadn't sampled, from the digging of a cable trench and the martialling of a ration party at Birr Cross Roads to putting a revolver bullet through the head of a German who was coming at him round a traverse with a bayonet. That first night and first stand-to had been predecessor to many nights of ghostly mystery. There had been other raids since that fearsome expedition led by Toler during the storm in June, when they had spent three hours hung up by machine guns inside the German wire, and Brains had been brought back with a leg he would never use again. He had met others since of the breed of Corporal Sugger, and ex-Regular soldiers, lead-swingers, quartermaster-sergeants and the like held no terrors now for him. He had learnt on the whole to appraise a man's value in the line in inverse proportion to the volume of his talk. Others beside poor Baggallay had gone from a cheery hour in his company, in billet or dug-out, to sudden death. He had seen others besides Sugger suddenly fall shrieking to the bottom of the trench or cower at the corner of a traverse crouching on the fire-step with their backs to the parapet.

There wasn't much in the way of trench warfare, or of the reactions of human beings to twentieth-century armaments, that anybody could tell him. He knew the anxiety which comes with the midnight hours of a moonless night, when one can see but ten yards ahead and some cheerful R.E. officer on his way back to Brigade has remarked that they are certain to attack. He knew that strange sympathy with the German infantry 200 yards away which one instinctively feels when the artillery of each side is registering upon front-line trenches. He knew what it means to stand in a fire-bay and curse the Staff,

PASS GUARD AT YPRES

the artillery, the A.S.C., the trench-mortar merchants, the next battalion, even the next company, everything, everybody but one's own forsaken little crowd. He knew, with Grenfell, those moments of exaltation which come, even if rarely, when the thundering line of battle stands. All this he knew, and one thing more, what it means to belong to a division and a battalion which is under a cloud, but which knows perfectly well that when the crisis came it did all that any division, Kitchener or Regular, could do. And this knowledge, and the knowledge of what terror means, the loss of comrades and disgrace to accompanying torturing death, had not broken him, but had left him pretty hardened and, as it appeared at the present moment, very much with his monkey up. They'd had their gruel, had they? Good enough! The best in their crowd had been wiped out, only 200 of the originals were remaining. Right. The Boche was still round Wipers, still looking at them from the hills to north and east and south. Just wait a bit, with the Mills bombs coming out, the new drafts being broken in, the battalion reshaped, shrapnel now unlimited and our artillery strengthening day by day. South Africa had started something like this, and—yes—he'd learnt a good deal from good old Bamford; let them wait.

Topping, these September nights, with the harvest moon. He pulled the flap of his doorway to one side, stepped out for a moment and looked around. Gad, it was good to be alive on a night like this. There were our star shells far away, now pretty well as good as theirs; those flashes were the flashes of our guns; and somewhere there, down at the end of a white road that faded into the moonlit distance, lay a town which stood for the frustration of many German hopes. Be damned to them all—the croakers at home, and the Staff, and the Boche, those swine at Corps H.Q. and all who'd tried to crab them and do them down: hadn't they helped to save their Wipers? And did the Boche imagine that there was nothing more to come, that his bombers and the whole battalion were being fattened for a Laffan's Plain review? There's Loos to come, he muttered with a smile: hope you enjoy it. Good-night, blasted Huns and other pretty darlings. Good-night, Ypres, old girl: sleep safe!

The iron had entered deep: it had not yet pierced to his inmost soul.

CHAPTER XVI

To say that Private Bamford was in any real sense elated would be an overstatement. The experiences of the past few months had only served to deepen his philosophy in regard to war, and he took the daily events of trenches or reserve billets without emotion as they came. Yet, on this occasion, one who could have read in secret places might have perceived a certain vague fluttering round Private Bamford's heart, not entirely dissimilar to if fainter than that rush of feeling that had come to him fifteen years before, when he stood at the foot of Glencoe to face his first engagement. Rumours he knew all about, and no rumour save of disaster lived long in Bamford's presence. But rumours and definite statements from G.H.Q. are different matters, and this was clear enough. They were going over the top that night, over and on and through. That meant, say, by November, the end of the war, which meant in its turn that he would qualify for his sixteen years' pension, and be nicely home for Christmas. Just see his officer through this last little bit, and that would be the end of that, if only he didn't do anything extra foolish and the bullet with his number didn't come. Wasn't any thanks to him, he must say, that it hadn't come already. Look at him now, talking to that Staff

fellow, head and shoulders over parapet, as if they were
looking over the Thames Embankment. He'd better go
and drop him a hint: no—as Private Bamford lumbered
a few steps forward and then drew quickly back—no, in
the circumstances, not. He always believed in lying low
while G.O.C.s were about, and here was the G.O.C. He'd
been just like that at Kimberley, he remembered; all this
damned keenness, that was what it was, and it didn't seem
as if he'd grown out of it since then. There they were now,
both of 'em at it; Freddy Mann leaning over and pointing
towards the lake, and the G.O.C. eagerly following his
finger. Ought to be at Division, as a matter of fact, the
G.O.C. They were going over three hours from now: he
supposed, though, he wanted to be in at the death. So
would he, if he were G.O.C. Bit of all right, to be a G.O.C.,
and know your whole blooming Division was going
through. None of that Redvers business this time. Lucky
swine, the G.O.C., to have a job like his, and know he
was top-dog over the Boche. Hullo, he was off now, with
Harry. Funny, that way he fell behind for a moment, and
looked back and tugged at his moustache as if he were
worried about something. Just a trick, that was all that
was; nothing much to worry about for him or anybody
else. The Boche was done: French had said so himself
in so many words in this special order that had just
come round. No earthly doubt about it, reflected Private
Bamford, as he contentedly spat pieces of plug into the
corner of the traverse: it can only mean one thing when
a General visits a front line trench twice in twenty-four

hours, and an officer gives his batman ten francs to buy chocolate at the first shop they come to, and tells him to keep the change. He'd just shove along now, and begin to get ready for it by scrounging the Q.M.S.'s rum.

·　　·　　·　　·　　·

The worst that could be said against General Vicke as a soldier and a Divisional Commander was that he was too attached to his men. This fault had been the subject of comment at Aldershot and was increasingly in evidence during the operations in Belgium in 1915. Care for one's men is, of course, inculcated as one of his first duties into the mind of every junior officer, and previously in South Africa and India General Vicke had shown that he had learnt his lesson to the full. When, however, one arrives at the rank of Major-General, and finds oneself in command of 12,000 infantrymen and gunners, to say nothing of mounted troops and details, care for the individual must to a certain extent be merged in considerations of strategy and of the unit as a whole. It was by this time sufficiently established that a division in such a sector as Ypres loses 60 per cent. of its strength every three months, and entirely changes its personnel, sometimes more than once, in a year.

The wise commander, in view of this, will therefore steel himself against undue interest in the subaltern or private soldier. His men cannot in the nature of things be to him as were Methuen's to their commander in

South Africa, or Roberts' at Kandahar. It was a pity that with all his excellent qualities General Vicke never quite appreciated this point. To have done so would have in no way conflicted with his well-established habit of slipping off whenever possible to the front-line trenches, and dropping into dug-outs to share a drink from flask or canteen with subalterns or men. He could have done this, and still known every officer and many N.C.O.'s by their names, while recognising without mental disturbance the fact that within a few weeks or at most months they were almost bound to part. As it was, as Corps Commanders and high Staff officers would remark, this damned paternal interest was all very well, but there was a war on, and you can't make omelettes without breaking eggs, and all this worrying about casualties upset corps commanders' equanimity and the peace of Army Conferences.

He was, it was recognised, getting on, was Vicke, and probably it was too late to change him now, but the Corps Commander didn't like it and it was rumoured that it was this defect alone that kept him from greater things than a divisional command. If he had dropped 10,000 in the Salient since April, well, so had others, that and more, and he would probably drop a damned sight more before he'd finished, so he'd better just make up his mind to it and cease to worry. Which was just what Archie Vicke refused to do. He would pore over casualty lists, ask who 24,218 of the Redjackets or 44,317 of the Southshires was, and whether he was married or single, and what sort of a wound he had had, and whether he had died in pain, and who had written to his relatives, and get hold of the A.D.M.S. and ask him whether it wasn't possible to save more lives, and criticise tactical plans submitted to him on the ground that they involved undue exposure to the men, and turn his R.E.s on to the building of shell-proof shelters for O.P.s even if it meant taking them away from their other work. As the Army Commander once remarked, the thing seemed always on his mind.

Some hoped that matters would improve after the flame attack, in which two of his brigades had practically been wiped out. But although he was always cheerful enough, as he stumped round the line in his blue reefer coat, or sat at the head of his mess-table in the evening, watching the port go round, August saw no real change, and this defect in his composition prevented his appreciating the beauty of the plan which involved the holding attack on September 25th at Ypres. Though he failed to realise it, his division really didn't fare so badly: their casualties were, of course, in excess of those estimated, but as this invariably proved to be the case there was nothing to be surprised at there. The division didn't gain any ground, but, as General Vicke guessed, it wasn't really expected to, and, more important, it didn't lose any, which, in view of the situation as it had appeared at 3.30 that afternoon behind Bellewarde Farm, was rather lucky. His own regiment did not disgrace itself again. The subaltern in whom he had been interested came through, after hanging on throughout the day and the greater part of the night with a little squad of men to a few sandbags and bits of timber which he called a trench by Witteport Farm, trying to keep a Lewis gun going with half the team knocked out, scrambling round the dead and wounded for ammunition, and praying that the death which seemed each moment more inevitable would be merciful and sudden when it came.

CHAPTER XVII

THIS was a Blighty all right. Private Beard lay in the shell-hole, waiting for the stretcher bearers, unable to believe his luck. Blighty, after all this time, and on a night like this. Those other poor swine, who'd been there when the shell burst in the middle of them, they hadn't got Blighties. Bartlett had just told him it had done them in. Lucky, he was, just now to get it, when he needed it most of all. He reached for the letter in his tunic pocket, which had told him of the new arrival. Boy this time, too—he'd see it before it was a fortnight old. Want a bit more light than this to see it by; couldn't see a yard ahead on a night like this. It had been as dark as pitch when they set out to build this emplacement, and it was even darker now. Day would be along soon, however; he supposed they'd take him in soon after daybreak. Mitchell had said as he tucked him away out of the way that they'd be along soon after daybreak. They'd have been along before, only after this attack they'd got so much to do. However, a bit of a wait didn't make any odds as far as he was concerned. What did a bit of pain matter, and a dull feeling in his forehead, when he'd clicked for home? Home, and those kids again.

Bit of a row going on, although from where he was he couldn't see any flashes. Day was a long time coming, but it would be, of course, after a night like this. Never known such a night: it didn't seem to matter whether he opened his eyes or shut them he couldn't see a thing. Pity the stretcher bearers were quite so busy; he couldn't help being a bit impatient; after all there was a new arrival waiting for him at home. Bit close, that last one, but a shell never dropped in the same hole twice: he was safe enough, even if he couldn't move and couldn't see a thing.

∙   ∙   ∙   ∙   ∙

"Go on, Bett, you tell 'im."

"Rather you did, mate; 'tain't my line. Suppose you're sure?" as if by an afterthought.

Bartlett nodded. He was sure enough: so, for that matter, was Bettson. They had wondered at four o'clock, when first the day was breaking; wondered more as the light grew clearer, and they had known at 5. And from then till now they had waited by the shell-hole, tending him as best they could, listening to his stories of home and the kids he was going to see so soon, and of this new young 'un, who was hardly a week old and was supposed to be so like his father. They had agreed that it wouldn't half be a bit of all right to see the kids again; that the kids wouldn't half be glad to see him, even if a bit was chipped out of his face and his arm was in a sling. They'd know him, and wouldn't he know them, too; even this new kid, he'd know him at once, though he was only about the size of a foot rule and he hadn't ever seen him; never mind that, he'd see him now soon enough. For two hours off and on he had talked, and they had sat there and agreed, praying all the time for the stretcher bearers to come. It couldn't last much longer; it couldn't go on for ever.

"Get longer, these 'ere nights, now summer's closing in, or p'raps it's longer when it's dark. 'Bout four o'clock now, suppose it'll be?"

" 'Bout that, mate. You lie still. They'll fetch yer soon."

"Been dozin' a bit; don't quite remember; 'ow long have I been 'ere in this 'ere 'ole?"

"Hour or two, p'raps; don't you bother yourself—not to talk too much."

"Aye, that's it. Difficult to tell the time, yer know, when you've 'ad a crack on the 'ead like me. Gawd, it wasn't half a burst, that shell; fair knocked me silly. Like lightning, it was, all round me 'ead. Made me eyes smart a bit, too, yer know."

"Better tell 'im, Bett. 'E's got to know. Thank Gawd, 'ere's the M.O. 'Ere y'are, sir, 'ere he is, all ready. Better take 'im quick."

The M.O. still retained something of a bedside manner. He was a stout fellow, done to the world himself after eighteen hours of duty on end; a day in the trenches followed by a night devoted to doing what he could to help those who had been done in when the German heavies got in to the "C" Company working party at Hooge. Casualties equal to twice the number of the battalion had already passed through his hands since May, but he still believed in keeping cheerful and in seeing that his patients shared his cheer. He came with his stretcher to the shell-hole, and bent over the wounded man.

"This him, is it? Sorry I'm late, but there's the devil of a mess at Hooge. Now get this bandage off, old son, and let's have a look at you; time to get up, you know."

"Bit early, ain't it?" Private Beard felt ready for a joke. "Who wants to get out o' bed at four o'clock?"

"Four o'—what in the world are you talking about? Six o'clock on a bright summer morning, that's what it is, me lad; quite long enough of sleep you've—— Hullo, what's up?"

"Six o'clock?" Beard's voice was cracked and ghastly. He put his hand quickly to his forehead.

"Yes, six. The sun's shining. Hullo——" The doctor bent down quickly.

Bettson and Bartlett moved away. There is no need for more than one to be at his side when a man has dreamed for months of his children's faces, and suddenly learns that night has given place to the full blaze of day, and still he cannot see.

CHAPTER XVIII

F REDDY MANN's own sympathies were all with Uncle
Wal. Uncle Wal had on more than one occasion in the
past few days expressed the opinion that the youngster
"would have had about enough of this 'ere war, and
wouldn't want all this talk about it while on leave." Nice
quiet day or so in the country, with a pub or two nearby,
then p'raps a show or so in Town to finish up with and
send him back cheerful-like—that was the best medicine
for him, according to Uncle Wal. The difficulty was that
no opinion expressed by Uncle Wal was likely to go down
in the Mann household, as Uncle Wal was suspect. He was
a rather excitable thin-faced man, with a reddish nose and
eyelids, who spent a good deal of his time, when staying
with his brother-in-law, in walking in and out between the
living-rooms and the shop, rubbing his hands or wiping
his moustache with a multicoloured handkerchief, and
asking every now and then with a snigger whether there
was long to wait till six o'clock. Not even now, when their
prayers had been answered and their dear son and his
nephew had been restored to them for a few days from
the horrors of war, could Uncle Wal be induced to behave
with fitting seriousness. He seemed to imagine that the
one thing their brave soldier wanted was to hang about

RONALD GURNER

with him half the morning and most of the evening in the parlour of the "Spotted Boar" or listen to the vulgarest jokes that could be picked up from the music-halls. It was a pity that his visit happened to coincide with Freddy Mann's arrival in October. However, they couldn't very well turn him out, and the others would see that Freddy Mann was treated more in the manner in which he deserved to be. The chief characteristic of this treatment consisted to all appearance in the manifestation of an overwhelming interest in everything that their poor boy had suffered, and from his arrival on Tuesday evening until the last day but one of his leave Freddy Mann had been kept steadily at it.

His father was not so difficult to deal with. All that was needed in his case was a large-scale map of Ypres with the British and German lines marked in pencils of various colours to illustrate the various changes of position. He would lean over this in an evening, after the table had been cleared, nodding his head in approval and remarking, "Yes, you're right, me boy, we're winning. Business as usual and the British bulldog spirit, that's what'll see us through." But the ladies of the household, the drove of aunts and cousins, whom he could always count on finding at Edenhurst, were more insistent in their demands for information. Aunt Jane, from Peckham, in particular was almost ghoulish. His dear mother had told her about some of the things he'd told her about in letters, apparently, but she couldn't believe such things could happen, she couldn't indeed, and it all went to show that as the dear minister

124

was saying in chapel last Sunday evening, it was a world given over to the works of iniquity and wickedness. But now he was here at last she'd be able to hear for herself and judge. Never mind about her feelings, she could bear it, she hoped, as well as any other good Christian woman; let him just go on and tell her exactly what it had been like in the trenches, that night when they had that awful raid, and something dreadful happened to that poor man's back and leg—or that day when so many men were burnt with that dreadful fire, and was that other poor man ever found, who'd been buried beneath a wall in Ypres, and would that man who had been struck blind that night never be able to see again?

Not that she always had things entirely in her own way, for Cousin Helen saw to that. Cousin Helen, not without reason, tended to regard Aunt Jane as a bit of an old humbug and a sentimentalist. Sitting there in the corner lapping up the horrors like a cat laps cream wasn't doing her or anybody else much good. Freddy Mann didn't want that sort of conversation; he wanted good sensible discussion upon the war as it was and upon what was likely to happen. Sensible conversation with Cousin Helen usually consisted in culling the maximum number of rumours or confidential information from any one source in a given time. She worked in a Government department in Whitehall where one's social value was to a large extent determined by the war stories and scandal which one could recount upon authority which one could vouch for. A live cousin, back on leave after five months in the Salient was too good an opportunity to be missed, and Cousin Helen made the most of her time. It was true, then, that the Division was off to Egypt. She had heard something about it, as that Nora Thompson's brother was in the Gunners, but you could never depend, of course, on anything that Nora Thompson said. She was glad to know for certain. Of course, she wouldn't breathe a word about it, but it was nice to know for certain. That was pretty true, she supposed, about the casualties: it was true, wasn't it, that they had lost 70,000 since May; it was said at the office that the losses at Loos had been so appalling that no reserves were left, and G.H.Q. were terrified of a break-through afterwards. Were those stories true, by the way, that they heard about G.H.Q.? She'd heard—well, she didn't like to repeat it, but Freddy Mann would know the stories that she meant. And what was the truth about these attacks? Was it the case that the men had to be made dead drunk on rum before they would go over the top?

The collection of information in this last head usually defeated its own ends, as it brought Aunt Emma on to the scene. It was extraordinary to Aunt Emma that dear Helen could talk dispassionately of such dreadful things as making the men drunk on rum. Surely she knew that that was just the sort of thing that the W.T.P.L. was trying to combat. The W.T.P.L. (Women's Temperance and Purity League, she snapped, in reply to Mr. Mann's very natural question) was just inquiring into this very matter; it was difficult to believe all that one was told about this and other things, but for dear Helen to sit there and talk about them all as natural was really too much. Surely she didn't imagine that that dear boy of theirs, with all the ideals for which he fought, would lend himself to anything so dreadful as making men drunk on rum. The Germans might do that sort of thing, but the idea that Englishmen fighting for liberty and all that was fine and noble—whence would follow the eternal argument between the idealist and the realist, not unadorned with personalities, during which Freddy Mann would slip off to see what his mother or Uncle Wal were about. He was at peace when with his mother, but she was rather eclipsed by the horde of relatives, and had little to say when they were alone except that she hoped they would send him to Egypt if it was safer there, and that she was glad that blow on the head in July hadn't done him any lasting harm, and that he must remember always to write to her, as his letters were all she had, and that Muriel was coming round that evening.

Yes, there were always the evenings to look forward to, when Muriel, sweet and demure as ever, would come round with her father. If only he could get her alone sometimes, without that father of hers always being about. On this Thursday evening, for example, when the special dinner in his honour was arranged, what the devil did he want to come round for, slapping him on the back and yapping about the heroism of the troops and the war of attrition. If you wanted heroes, you didn't want attrition, as Freddy Mann told him forcibly enough over dessert, in language inspired by a sudden memory of Kaye in a mess at Watou. John Farrant was no doubt somewhat taken aback, but he'd started it and he'd have to lump it.

"Come on, Muriel," Freddy Mann said almost roughly, as he left the room. "Come into the garden. I want to talk to you."

How sweet she looked as she slipped her scarf round her shoulders and tripped by his side down the steps.

"You know, Muriel, I'm sorry if I was rude to your father, but he doesn't know what this war is."

"Oh, Fred!"

"Well, he doesn't, and what's more, there doesn't seem to be anybody in this bl—— in Edenhurst who does."

Muriel's eyes gleamed in sympathy, as she looked at him in the moonlight.

"Oh, Fred, what you must have suffered!"

" 'Tisn't anything to do with what I've suffered." Freddy Mann made a quick gesture of impatience. "It's all this footling talk. Either we're ninepins, millions of us on either side, to be knocked down to see which side has the last one left, or we're stained-glass heroes with haloes round our heads."

"But aren't you heroes? We all think——"

"Dunno—if heroes curse the Staff and the A.S.C. and the day they were born or were fools enough to join the Army, and leap with joy when they get Blighties, and drink like fishes out of water when they get a chance, and—God, what's the use of talking?"

He stopped a moment, and pulled fiercely at his pipe.

"Everybody's so nice about it here. Your father's so nice about the way we've all got to stand up on both sides and allow ourselves to be killed, and Aunt Emma's so nice about our morals and ideals, and Helen fits us all into nice little pigeon-holes according to whether we're good, useful soldiers or bad, and—— Suppose we ought to be sitting up all night, according to them, thinking about whether we've said our prayers and who's going to win the war. I don't know who's going to win the war. Don't suppose anybody ever will win the war. Don't suppose it'll ever stop. And I don't care either, about that or anything else, so long as——"

"Oh, Fred!"

"Well, I don't. What's the use of telling lies. I don't. Nor would your father, nor would any of the whole pack of 'em, if they'd had six months at Wipers. Does you in, does Wipers. Done our crowd in, anyway. Damned few of us left now, and those that are don't care. Different before Loos or July, perhaps—but now——"

He suddenly looked at Muriel. She was beautiful indeed—gold hair, gleaming eyes——

"Be damned to the lot of them. I don't want their talk or sympathy. There's only one thing I care about, that's——"

Hot with passion, he seized her, and covered her face and neck with kisses.

"You."

He went on kissing. The more he kissed, the more he wanted to. Go on—her eyes now, and her throat, and——

"FRED!" as she finally wrenched herself away. "Oh——" She burst into copious tears. "Oh, Fred, I didn't believe you could—behave like that."

"But damn it, Muriel, what the——"

"We aren't engaged, you know, Fred. Father says we're too young. And, even if we were, that isn't the way to kiss."

Freddy Mann stood for a moment in unfeigned astonishment. "You don't mean to say, Muriel, you're angry."

"No, Fred, not angry, but very hurt. I did believe in you so. I—it makes me all hot. I——"

The tears flowed freely.

"I didn't think you could ever have been like that. You were never like that before. It must be the war that's done it. To think that you ever thought that I was that sort of girl."

"Oh, God! Oh, my giddy aunt!" Freddy Mann groaned.

"I'll try to forget it, Fred. But please, please, oh please—I thought it was ideals you fought for, and the protection of the weak and women. You don't seem yourself any longer. Just a brute. It's such bad manners to kiss a girl like that."

·   ·   ·   ·   ·

Uncle Wal was at Victoria Station to see him off. This was the last thing in the world that Freddy Mann expected, as he had most carefully explained that he had suddenly found that he had to leave the night before. It was a great pity, he agreed, but it just couldn't be helped, and he particularly didn't want anybody to bother to come to London with him. Yet there was Uncle Wal, standing at the entrance to the platform, wiping his moustache as usual. Freddy Mann stopped short. The situation was a little difficult.

"That's all right. It's only me. It's only old Uncle."

"But what——?"

"That's all right. Not opening time yet, you know," with the usual snigger.

"But, Uncle——"

Freddy Mann looked at his companion.

"Thought you might be mistaken, you know. In the railway line meself, and I happen to know about these 'ere leave trains, so I guessed somehow that you might be mistaken."

The three stood silent. Uncle Wal glanced from his nephew to the pretty girl by his side.

"Good morning, miss. Never you mind me. It's only old Uncle Wal. Thought I'd like, somehow, just to see him off. He said nobody was to come, but I just thought——"

He turned to Freddy Mann and took him by the arm aside a moment.

"You're right, lad. That lot there, they're enough to do you down. Wouldn't listen to me, of course. And that gal Muriel, she came the icicle, eh what?"

"Well?"

"I knowed her. She would. I knows 'em all. You're right."

He looked again to the companion.

"He's leaving us, missy. We'll wish him luck."

"We—I do. You'll come, Freddy, soon?"

"That's it. You tell him to come and he'll come. Ah well." He wiped his moustache again. "Getting near openin' time

131

now, and I mustn't keep yer. But 'ope yer didn't mind me just comin' for a moment. And—if yer'll just accept this in memory of yer old uncle." He pressed a cigarette case into his hand. "All these 'ere stories about cigarette cases and such stoppin' bullets. Well, glad to 'ave seen yer, me dear. Good-bye, lad—God—bless——"

Opening time had apparently come quickly. Freddy Mann watched the insignificant form shuffling away. He turned to one who had not denied him kisses. Time for a few more—just a few.

"Thank Bill, dear, for telling you of me."

"I will."

"You were happy, dear, last night?"

A kiss in answer.

"You'll write?"

Another kiss.

"You must go now, dear. But I shall be here when you come back. I'll—you know what I am, but——"

"Be damned to that."

"No use pretending"—with a forced and sudden laugh. "You know all right, but—I'm glad you came—goodbye—goodbye."

Back to the unknown. But he went as a soldier, not ill-content. He was as good as the next man, whoever he might be, speeding across the seas to war. He, too, for that last night had found companionship.

CHAPTER XIX

THERE are more cheerful experiences than that of returning to mess on a dull November day, after a long walk during which the Adjutant has explained in the greatest detail the arrangements which are being made to recall all winter clothing and equipment, and to issue khaki drill, sun helmets and shorts, and of discovering after all that the Division is not going to Egypt. Harry's beak nose and dirty briar pipe had never looked more ugly than when he passed the formal communication stating that all previous orders were cancelled and that the battalion would be prepared to return to the Ypres sector in two days. It was a damned uncomfortable mess, as Freddy Mann had always said. The tea was cold and the stove wasn't working. The rain hadn't stopped for a week, and there was no reason now to think that it would ever stop. The whisky had run out and he was sick of the lot of them: Bill with his swagger, Harry with his filthy temper, and Chips, who thought he'd known all about it and wasn't so damned clever after all. However, there was no point in grizzling, and as they had to go back to the northern sector Freddy Mann was rather glad that he was detailed next day to make the preliminary tour with Robbie. It happened to be fine, and they decided to start in the early hours so as to get a drink or two at Proven on the way. Impressions by 2 p.m. were favourable. They raised a lunch out of Toler, who was now at Corps and rather gave them to understand that he had bought the Château and no small part of the surrounding countryside.

They continued their journey in the afternoon through little lanes and unscarred woods to Brielen, and even after that through comparatively civilised country to Salvation Corner. By this time the northern sector of Ypres seemed well worth a visit. The dug-outs between the Yper and the Yperlette, which had never yet been shelled, were distinctly to be preferred to the filthy line of burrows by the ramparts. Coney Street was a very reasonable trench, and there seemed nothing to complain of when Robbie and Freddy Mann finally arrived, just as dusk was setting in, at the little circle of closely screened dug-outs which marked B.H.Q. at La Belle Alliance Farm. It promised to be an interesting sector. There were farms about, such as Frascati Farm and Wilson's Farm, which were still quite habitable, although they were practically within the lines. The Hun, to all accounts, was quiet, and the only matter for regret was that it was not possible to get to the front line past Forward Cottage by daylight. The main point was that they seemed at last to have got clear of Ypres: they approached to the north of it, and they wouldn't have to go on dodging Jack Johnsons and 5.9s in the square for the rest of their days.

Finally, after a dinner with Brigade near Essex Farm, Robbie and Freddy Mann started back, lorry-jumping to the Château des Trois Trois and getting a lift in a divisional car from there to St. Jan-ter-Biezen. Robbie, who for a latter-day saint could do himself quite well on occasion, was rather inclined to be philosophical and chatty. Freddy Mann quietly read a letter from Irene Terry, which he had thrust into his pocket just before they started, enjoyed the night, and concluded that all was for the best, that in all probability Egypt would have been a stinking mass of flies, and that one could find a reasonably decent war here without going further afield to look for it.

The mess was empty when they returned at midnight, except for Harry and one of the new arrivals, Guy Cadell, a well-intentioned young man who had been at pains to explain for the last few days that he was "public school," that he had joined the Southshires because it was a gentleman's regiment, and that the one thing he was living for was "to have a whack at the Boche." Robbie, after a final blow in the bowl of his pipe, announced that he was full of good whisky, and he thought the best thing to do was to make the best of it by going to bed and letting it go nicely to his head. Freddy Mann felt sleepy, but disinclined to turn in. He sat in the one vacant chair in the little room, idly sipping a whisky and soda and looking round him. Pity now that it had come to an end, that they had to leave this place. For six weeks, ever since the division had been taken out to refit, Watou had been their home, and there had been peace in Watou: parade drill which in its unreality almost reminded him of the

far-gone days in Aldershot, walks with Robbie, Harry
or Bill through little country lanes, past wayside shrines
to small towns and villages where few, if any, echoes
of war had to all appearance penetrated, long evening
hours in the café at the corner of the square, dinners
with the Yeomanry and with neighbouring companies
and battalions, and at night sleep—sleep, above all,
sleep—no fitful dozing broken by thoughts of "gas alert"
or of the sudden crash of some midnight shell, but a
sinking of one's body upon a pillow and a feather bed,
and oblivion till day. This very room, which bore signs
of something more than the usual fleeting occupation,
was associated in his mind with the best days that the
war had brought them since they left their kindly home
at Eperlecques. Between the crude oleographs of saints
upon the walls, interspersed with the inevitable pages
of *La Vie Parisienne*, Robbie and himself had hung one
or two pictures of their own—photographs of groups,
an engraving of Oxford and another of Edenhurst
Castle, even a copy of Dante and Beatrice to please Bill's
sentimental tastes. The table in the corner was even
more heaped than usual with map cases, field-glasses,
smoke helmets, literature of all sorts and kinds, old
tobacco tins, pipes, packs of cards, ink, writing pads and
bottles of Johnnie Walker. He had grown accustomed
to seeing Harry, head sunk deep down between his
shoulders, glowering genially in his arm-chair, or Bill
playing interminable games of patience and cursing
softly to himself the while. Yes, damned sorry to go. He

got up, shook himself, grunted goodnight to Harry, and made his way to bed. Two days. And then, with a look of kindly scorn at Guy Cadell as he paused a moment at the door, "You'll have your whack at the Boche all right, you blighter, and I hope you get your bellyful."

CHAPTER XX

THE bell of the Monastery St. Sixte tolls at midnight, and the monks of St. Sixte go to pray. At 3 in the morning the bell tolls, and they pass to their prayers again. It is their bell to which they hearken, their bell, their priest's voice, and no other sounds but these. Guns may be ranged round their monastery and shells pass overhead; soldiers may come and live for days or weeks within their walls, rejoicing in the comfort of their barns and beds, but to them these things are nothing. This war is no war of theirs; these matters for which men fight are matters which they have put far from them in the purification of their hearts. They pass, each on his way from cell to chapel, chapel to refectory, refectory back to cell, in silent communion and silent prayer. There is one among them who must speak with the outside world to satisfy their carnal needs, and he, whether the stranger be beggar or wandering penitent or soldier, will care for his needs as well as theirs. With him let these strangers speak: for themselves they speak to no man, they owe allegiance under God to one alone, their Abbot; they move, not to a trumpet, but to the tolling of a bell. These soldiers who come from the west today to pass to the east tomorrow, who have passed so far a winter and a summer and a winter, will pass to whatever destiny they may. But to themselves, to those of the silent brotherhood, these destinies are nothing. For them the bell, the watches at midnight, the *via dolorosa* and the peace unspeakable: what is it to them if their bell calls to other hearts besides their own, if a peace falls sometimes within their walls upon others, who, carnal perhaps and unregenerate, nevertheless must make offering, they too, of their bodies, and tread like them the way of pain?

·   ·   ·   ·   ·

As to others, so to the 6th Battalion Southshires the Monastery St. Sixte was the gateway to the east, to a life the nature of which they knew. It was impossible for them to remain long at St. Sixte, removed by fields and woods from war and even from their fellow men, the guests of a community which held no intercourse with them or with any of the outside world, but which moved day and night through gardens and corridors like ghosts in shrouds of russet brown. There was peace, indeed, for a day or two more, peace in secluded hutments among woods, or in tents on the road to Brielen: peace of a kind even in that line of dug-outs between the Yper and the Yperlette, where one could stand in perfect safety at the doorway and watch the shelling of Essex or Talana Farm fifty yards away across the road. But once over the canvas-screened bridges, and the road ended as all roads to the east must end, as elsewhere, so here, in a water-logged trench in the middle of a fœtid field. For those who defend Ypres, whether from north or east or south, the lot is equal. Forward Cottage for Bellewarde Farm, the Willows for Railway Wood—there is not much in it when you take over a sector in the Salient on a moonless night in driving rain.

"Think you've done Wipers down, do you? Have a drink and think again."

Why the devil, thought Freddy Mann, just now of all times, when he was staggering blindly round unknown sapheads with Robbie, must a picture of a pleasantly grinning officer dance suddenly before his eyes, or that other picture, of a peasant woman sitting in the sunlight, talking to him as to a child that had much to learn.

"It is always Ypres, *mon Bébé*. Always at the end is Ypres."

CHAPTER XXI

YOU will not escape, in the northern sector of the Ypres Salient, the High Command Redoubt. Stand upon the sloping bank to the east of the Yper, and you will see the solid wall of sandbags which compose it stand huge and menacing, from the Pilkem Ridge to Wieltje, dominating in its entirety the low ground between the German position and the mud-soaked British lines. Make your way across the fields to La Brique or Friscate Farm, creep up a broken stairway and look through the rafters of the attic, or stand in the front-line trenches beyond Forward Cottage, periscope in hand, and its sinister mass will fill the landscape. C.R.A.s will plot its course upon squared maps, and direct shoots upon C. 15, A. 33, or C. 14, B. 47; Stokes Mortar officers will select some machine-gun emplacement or noted dugout for their daily ration; an aeroplane flying low will bomb it along its length, but the next day it will be restored and remain impregnable, crowned with its fringe of stakes and wire, as the Germans intended when they built it that it should remain. Elsewhere, at Zillebeke perhaps or Hooge, the trenches opposite may, if at a cost, be taken. Here you may plaster the ridge from end to end with high explosive, and send men forward as you will, but your living waves will break upon unyielding rock, and at the end of the day those who built the High Command Redoubt will be masters of the ridge. You will, if you are wise, keep quiet within your trenches here. They will shell you on most days between 11 and 12, and 3 and 4, and you will bury your dead and send your casualties down in the daily convoy past Essex Farm to the dressing station at Salvation Corner; they will watch your goings and comings and smile from their fastness upon your impotence, but you are there to do no more than hold the Salient, and so long as you are at Mortaldje Estaminet and Turco Farm there will still be two good miles between the High Command Redoubt and Ypres. Issue your sheep-skin coats, your cardigans and your smoke helmets, take over and give up your thigh-boots, keeping strict tally of them as you enter or leave your sector, wrest from the mud what dry places you can for trenches and dug-outs, repair your revetments as they collapse, guard your men from lice and frost-bite—do all these things yourself, but leave your situation report to your sergeant or sergeant-major to compose: he will do it as well as you, for there will be nothing new to say.

You may last May have dreamt of an early advance, and have written to say that you expect with luck to be home by Christmas; but now, if you have a soul left, guard it in patience, for it is Christmas now, and now you know. Winter will turn again to summer, and the days will lengthen and shorten to another Christmas, and still another summer will follow before you take the Pilkem Ridge. Only some of your company will be there to see it: for yourself, you may be there, or there may be some other in your place. You thought, when you joined, you could do something: you know now that you can do nothing worth the doing. It was to Ypres, good fool, that you were glad to come last summer: here, at Ypres, where the High Command Redoubt is master, in bondage you will perforce remain.

CHAPTER XXII

"BUT, Bill, for God's sake——"
"I can't. Do what you like, I can't."

Freddy Mann looked at Bill, cowering furtively within the darkness of the dug-out.

"But, Bill, old chap, I say——"

Bill came grovelling a little forward. He stretched out his hand and pulled Freddy Mann towards him.

"Tell you——" His hands and head were shaking. "Something's gone—my head or legs. Can't you understand? I can't. Why don't they come and shoot me? God, these shells. I can't——"

Freddy Mann looked quickly along the trench. The men were all ready for patrol. The order had gone out for sentries not to fire. Townroe would be along at any moment now, to see them off. Then what the hell——

"I say, Bill, old chap, remember that first merry raid of ours? Up at Y Wood, you remember. Damned sight worse than this—you remember, old chap, eh?"

"Tell you——" Bill's voice rose to a hysterical note, then sank to a moan. "I can't—what's the use of trying?"

"Oh, Bill, for God's sake, Bill—the men are looking—— What the devil do you want, Cadell?"

"Just came to say that——" Guy Cadell looked at the huddled officer with a puzzled expression. "Anything up?"

"Nothing. Just giddy a moment, that's all. Better get—no don't—oh, go to Hell, it's nothing."

Guy Cadell stood still, anxious to help. He was new to the war, and he was still always anxious to know what was on and help.

"Why don't you go to Hell—no, go and ask Chips to come here a moment; then go to Hell if a shell doesn't get you first."

This seemed more definite, and Guy Cadell departed upon his complicated errand. Freddy Mann stood over Bill, and spoke almost in a tender and caressing voice.

"But are you sure? You know what it means. Come on, try. Let me help you up."

"I can't—it's gone—I can't."

"All ready for patrol, sir." Sergeant Mitchell's face appeared for a moment at the doorway.

"Right, just coming." Freddy Mann looked quickly at Bill, then at the parapet and the incessant bursts outside. Last hope.

"You can't?"

Bill whined and moaned. He was cowering further into the dug-out. In the light of a shell his face was green, and his eyes were like an animal's. Last hope. In a minute Townroe would be here, and it would be too late. His hand moved to his pistol.

"You can't—or won't?"

RON A LD GU RNER

"Oh." Bill covered his eyes. He tried to rise and fell back, as the dug-out rocked with a sudden explosion. Freddy Mann watched.

"Well?"

"I tell you——"

"Hullo, you chaps!" Chips Viner glanced at the revolver in Freddy Mann's hand. "Just priming up, eh? Well, I say, that damned patrol's off. C.O. thinks the night's a bit too thick. Stand the men down, if I were you, and then turn in. There's nothing else on. Got your situation report done, eh?"

"Yes."

"Well." He stooped and looked inside. "That you, Bill? Well, your special dish is off tonight. Never mind, we'll fix one up for you tomorrow. Cheerio, pip, pip."

Bill crawled forward when the two were left alone.

"I say—does he mean it?"

Slowly Bill got to an erect position in the trench before the dug-out. As if by habit he carefully replaced the sheet, then turned uncertainly to Freddy Mann.

"You know, I wish to God Chips hadn't come. I wish to God you'd shot. I'm done—here, give it to me."

He made a sudden grab for the pistol. Freddy Mann got him by the neck.

"Don't be a fool. Turn in. You'll be all right tomorrow. And for the Lord's sake stop that whining." He spoke impatiently.

Bill cowered by the dug-out, looking helplessly at him. His jaw was hanging loose, and he was slobbering.

"Thought you were a sport, Freddy Mann. Thought you were a pal of mine. 'Tisn't much for a pal to do, to shoot a fellow when he asks."

·   ·   ·   ·   ·

Freddy Mann ought to have taken Chips's advice and turned in. When one has been for five weeks in and out of the Kaye salient, and between Brielen, Essex Farm and the Mortaldje Estaminet, and is due as far as can be seen for another week at least, it is a pity not to take all the sleep that one can get. The patrol was called off. Good enough. Why not turn in instead of hanging about here alone in an abandoned traverse, looking at the dimly-seen High Command Redoubt towering in front of them and the waste of morass between them. Freddy Mann might have known what would come of it, even if Bamford had not reminded him once again that the only thing to do was to take things as they were, and he'd find a spot of rum on his side of the dug-out. Perhaps, though, it was difficult for him to know, for an utter weariness of flesh and soul comes only seldom to any man, and not usually to a boy who has not yet reached his twentieth year. It came, too, when Freddy Mann was not expecting it: quite suddenly, when peace had fallen and when nothing stirred beside him in the trench or in front of him in No Man's Land. Quite suddenly, that stench of death that was always in his nostrils seemed to enter his inmost being. Death, death—was there anything in the world but skeletons in shell-holes or on wire, any thought left to think but the thought of death, any hope in life but that of keeping death for twenty-four hours at bay, any object but that of dealing death by bullet or grenade? If only you could have death without this filthy stink. But no, death was a foul thing, and it was death, whether at Hooge, Zillebeke or Forward Cottage, that filled their days and nights. Here, as always, death's reek was round him: he would never be free of it again. In savage blind passion he half climbed on to the parapet and looked around him to Foch Farm upon his left, the Willows behind him, the dark mass upon his right which he supposed was Ypres. To think that saving Ypres, winning the war, protecting Belgium or doing any other of the damned silly things that they told him he was doing, had ever meant anything to him! To think that of his own free will he had put life on one side and given himself to this! Damned little they'd told him of what it was like, or he wouldn't have been here now. They'd talked about the regiment, and comradeship: they hadn't told him that a comradeship of six may in a few weeks become a memory in the mind of one alone, that a regiment, a battalion, a company of which one had grown proud may become within four months a crowd of indifferent strangers. They'd talked to him of courage: he hadn't known that not only a man's body, but his very spirit and soul could be broken, as Bill's—brave, laughing, fearless Bill's—had been broken in those last weeks in front of Ypres. They'd told him of God, they came and preached to him about God's service, as if they fondly imagined that he was fool enough to believe that God could remain in Heaven and see the torture that men wrought and suffered on earth.

Was there any lie they hadn't told him, any lie that six months ago, poor fool, he would not have believed? He'd paid, that's all, he'd paid: and he was through. He wasn't like Robbie, who could go on calmly, smoking his pipe, rescuing wounded men by daylight, treating the heaviest bombardment as if it were nothing more than a storm of rain. Robbie might have some inner secret to support him: he hadn't. He knew now that this stink of death was all that life meant to him, or could ever mean. It had got most of the others, had death: it would get him soon enough. Why not—he laughed and raised himself a little higher on the parapet—why not save it trouble? He didn't want to die in agony, his guts dropping out and his blood pouring out of a hole the size of a pudding plate like Martin's. He didn't want to crack, like Bill had cracked. He'd just had enough, and he wanted to slip away. It was so easy, too—just a walk along the canal bank past Essex Farm and Hull Farm towards Boesinghe, where the German lines drew to the canal, on and on, with the light breaking, till it came; or a walk from Foch Farm, out towards the Pilkem Ridge—there wouldn't be more than five yards there to go; or in daylight, over Hilltop Farm, or past Forward Cottage over the ridge towards the line; or, simpler still, just over and through the wire, and then on through the marshes till you came to the High Command Redoubt; or, without bothering to walk at all, this pistol—all those fellows out there were peaceful enough, and they didn't care now whether they stank or not. Why go on, when all you had to live for was to crawl like a hunted rabbit through mud, and see bloody fools who came to you from time to time and told you you were saving Ypres? Why, come to that—he laughed aloud, and looked behind him. Ypres was dead. They'd never told him that, but it was; just bones, like the bones out there. Let the dead look after the dead, the dead could guard Ypres well enough. George Harvey had said that—let——

"Now, if you'll let me 'ave it, sir, I'll just clean your pistol."

Was anybody alive then? Funny, that dear old Bamford was still alive.

"You don't want to 'old it, not like that you don't, in case—just you let me 'ave it, sir. An' the tot o' rum's still there, and it's time for a bit of a turn in—there's two hours yet before stand-to. Bit done up, sir, that's what it is. I remember when I was with Methuen at Magersfontein——"

That wasn't death carrying him. It was Bamford, at least it sounded like Bamford's voice.

"We're agoin' out tomorrow, sir—just 'eard—bit o' rest. That's it—just let me get me arm round these boots o' yours. That's it. Let's just 'ave yer arm over me shoulder. Out tomorrow, and the bullet ain't come yet. Now 'ere's yer dug-out and 'ere's the officer what sent me for yer—no you don't want to go that way, sir, towards the sap 'ead—turn right the dead, turn left the livin'—that's it, sir—must have 'is joke, must Bamford."

He looked across the now limp form to Robbie.

"Comes o' thinkin', sir. All in, 'e is. What's the use o' thinkin' in this 'ere war? Either we'll be cold mutton tomorrow, or we won't."

Bamford was right. It is a mistake to go and stand in a trench alone at midnight, amid the stench of a thousand corpses, and listen to shells, and moans and think.

CHAPTER XXIII

THAT was the worst part over. As usual he and Robbie had managed to pull it off. Patrols always seemed to go right when he was with Robbie. It didn't matter how often the German star-shells rose flickering in the air to throw a sudden whiteness over No Man's Land and fall to the earth apparently just beside them, so long as Robbie's angular features and blunt almost bullet-like head were near him as they lay doggo in grass or shell-hole. Robbie was just the fellow for the game: Harry's temper tended to be a bit trying in No Man's Land, and most of the others, like Barnes or Cadell, were about as much use as babes unborn. But it was a different thing with Robbie: if poor Bill had been going out with Robbie he wouldn't have cracked the way he had: he wouldn't have cracked either, if he had known it was going to be an easy job like this. Here was the opening, straight in front of them, with nobody apparently in the sap-head by its side, and very little wire. All they would have to do when they came over next week would be just to walk through, spend as long as they liked on the advanced trench, and then come quietly home. Anyway, they'd done their bit tonight. Pity all jobs in No Man's Land weren't as soft as this. Times without number they'd been chivvied home with machine guns and grenades. There was hardly a bullet about tonight, and as for shells or bombs—ah, there was that Mortaldje Estaminet machine gun getting busy; it often did, about this time. Didn't really matter, as from where they were the bullets were all overs. However, here was a shell-hole handy, and there was plenty of time to go. Only two hundred yards back, and five hours before daylight. They'd stop here for a bit: it was a good-sized hole with plenty of room for both of them. They'd done their job, and they could easily get back when the machine-gun fellow stopped. A good sort of patrol altogether; the best they'd been on since they came to the northern sector; the sort of job that brought back something of the old thrill, and almost made the war worth while. His first patrol had been with Robbie: if only it could be with Robbie to the end. They'd got through one more patrol together, anyway. Nothing could very well go wrong tonight.

·   ·   ·   ·   ·

The German trench mortar officer lazily bestirred himself and moved from his dug-out to the parapet. He grunted as he moved, as he objected to these disturbances. This new Colonel of theirs, this Bavarian fusspot, was always imagining figures and movements in No Man's Land where none existed: he was perfectly capable of mistaking a stake for a fixed rifle or a line of willows for a patrol. Fussy devil. There wasn't any noise and there wasn't anything moving at the bottom of the redoubt.

However, there wasn't any point in making a row about it. If the Colonel said there was something there, he'd better poop one off and think no more about it. He idly let off two grenades, looked round the redoubt and the marshes in front of them with a full appreciation of their position, let off a third for luck and turned in to sleep till dawn.

CHAPTER XXIV

FREDDY MANN wished he wouldn't talk so much. The only thing he asked was to be allowed to lie quiet on the stretcher, now that the shelling had stopped. He didn't want to move, because that hurt his shoulder, and he didn't want to hear how this fellow had stopped his packet, or exchange confidences or cigarettes. But he was a persistent customer, this "wounded 'ero" as he insisted on calling himself with a grin; a cheerful undersized Cockney subaltern, whose natural optimism was accentuated by the possession of what he termed "a Blighty that he wouldn't exchange for fifty quid."

"No, nor for £100 I wouldn't," he continued, "£100 *and* drinks included. Here, old sport, you try one o' these. Trois Maisons, that's what we calls 'em at the Ritz. Talk about Blighties——" He lifted his bandaged arm. "Talk about a bit o' luck. Smashed bone, and two nerves gone, but elbow untouched. Nine months to heal, the doctor bird says, but nothing permanent—what d'yer think o' that? Last lap. Get us away from this 'ere Wipers, and there we are. Shifting us tonight at 7—then Pop, and Watou—oh, what-ho for Watou (ha, ha, good one that) and carry me back to Blighty. Gawd's own luck, I calls it." He nodded his head in general recognition of the fortune that had come his way.

"That's just what it is with Blighties, yer know, all luck. Feller, for example, next to me when that crump bust last night—Johnson, the Q.M. bloke—he was talking about Blighties and what he'd pay for one, same as one does when up in them blooming trenches. He says he'd take a leg Blighty for £25—just says it natural, talking, same as we're talking now, and the crump comes and takes 'em both off, clean above the knee. Going a bit strong, that. Still, it's what he said. What he asked for he got. But as for me——"

Silence for a moment, while he screwed himself round on his stretcher to look at Freddy Mann.

"You've done rather well, mate, too, ain't yer? Shoulder, ain't it?"

"Yes."

"Walking case, ain't yer?"

"Suppose so, but I bled a bit and they shoved me here."

"Yes; oh well, no complaints—not like 'im." He jerked his finger to the dying man who was moaning on the stretcher to his right. "Half his chest blown away, that R.A.M.C. feller tells me—all up for 'im. But as for us—once they gets us out of 'ere and on the road to Pop—— What 'appened?" With a sudden interest. "Chance crump, or was yer asking for it?"

"Half and half. Patrol, you know. Usual sort of thing. Got us by the wire in front of the High Command Redoubt. Thought it was a soft job, too, that was the funny thing about it. They spotted us and sent a bomb or something over and got me. Other fellow took five hours to get me back. I was unconscious half the time."

156

"Um—ah—yes," replied the Blighty specialist. "Yes, that's good enough—ought to be able to make something of a tale out of that for the pretty darlings that'll nurse yer. Deck it up a bit, shells crashing round, knee deep in blood, yer know. Expect a bit o' colour, do the sweet little bits at home. Damned glad, I suppose you are, like me?"

"Well I suppose I am—dunno."

"What d'yer mean—'dunno'? How long 'ave yer been out?"

"Six months—no, seven."

"You must be glad, then. Three times as long as me, that is, and I'm glad enough. Back to the gels at 'ome— you got a gel at 'ome?"

"Yes." Curse the fellow, couldn't he shut up? The chap on his left was dying, and he wanted to get to sleep, if his shoulder would give him half a chance. Of course he was glad. Why shouldn't he be? Why worry about Harry and Robbie and Chips, and his own crowd, Mitchell, Bartlett, Bettson, and, yes, old Bamford. He knew they'd have to pass on one day. Most of them had faded away before. How he'd prayed for this, like everybody else he'd ever met. Hadn't he cursed the very sight of Wipers? Well, he was leaving Wipers now. It was Blighty now. Of course he was glad—damned glad.

"Course you're glad—and if you've got a gel at home——"

Of course he'd got a girl at home: he'd said so once. Why couldn't he stop, and let him go to sleep?

"Fact of the matter is, old son, we're damned lucky, you and I. Anybody's lucky to get out of this show alive. Only thing to do, if you're fool enough to have come out, is to get back p.d.q. We've pulled it off, old feller. Damned lucky, ain't we, eh?"

He was right, after all; that was what it all came to. Never mind the hopes with which you once marched eastward, never mind the comradeship, days in billets with Harry, nights in No Man's Land with Robbie, never mind the rot you believed in when first you came: and as for Ypres—get out of it, if possible, alive. He was right, but why the devil couldn't he shut up, instead of harping on the truth?

"Funny," the Irrepressible continued, as he raised himself on his stretcher and looked around. "Deuce of a lot you can see from here, now the sun's come out a bit. There's Salvation Corner, down there, and that's the St. Jean road, just up there to the left, and there's the line just over there. Be able to see the flashes, we will, when the sun's gone down."

Freddy Mann lay still. He didn't want to see the flashes of the guns across the ridge, or the battalions marching to the trenches, or the torn poplars by the wayside. He'd had enough.

"And there's old Wipers. That's the Cloth Hall, that is. That's the tower."

Freddy Mann drew himself down lower on the stretcher and shut his eyes. Wipers, was it? He didn't want to see Wipers or the Cloth Hall any more. He was tired, and he wanted sleep.

CHAPTER XXV

IT was an obvious mistake upon the part of the appropriate military authority to allow Dick Leverett to mix with the other inhabitants in Millfield Hospital. Such an oversight was in marked contrast with the devoted care with which in all other respects the interests of the patients were watched. The wounded officer could not in most matters affecting his moral welfare complain of negligence or indifference. He was relieved of all responsibility for protecting himself from the pitfalls of the night by the simple regulation that he had to be within the hospital by 10 p.m. As dancing is in so many cases the first step downhills, he was categorically forbidden to dance within the military area of the Metropolis. Lest, by a simple subterfuge, he should escape observation when engaged upon nefarious pursuits, he was forbidden to wear mufti upon any occasion. In order that no insidious slackness might undermine his efficiency as a soldier, he would rise to stand as best he could at the foot of his bed at attention when the Colonel carried out his morning tour of inspection. Conversation with sisters or nurses was not encouraged: a watchful eye was kept upon his visitors. The number of restaurants, caves and dug-outs which were out of bounds at any given moment tended, particularly in the heart of London, to exceed those which he was allowed to enter. It was considered desirable that he should not leave the hospital premises till twelve o'clock, in order that the best hours of the day should be devoted to contemplation of the management of the ward and the sufferings of those more seriously wounded than himself. Care, and more than care, was taken, but no system can be faultless and it must remain as one blot upon an otherwise excellent record of surveillance that Dick Leverett, full charged with his ideas and views, "got abroad" at Millfield in the second summer of the war.

By an odd perversity of genius, Dick Leverett managed to turn many of the best-meant rules and regulations displayed so prominently in the entrance hall to his own fell purposes. Those long mornings of dead monotony, and evenings enlivened only by bridge and the narration of innumerable non-drawing-room stories of an advanced description, gave him his chance, and when Dick Leverett saw his chance he took it. He was a cadaverous individual, not conspicuously military in appearance, who spoke in a rather thick, blurred voice and whose words were accompanied by nervous gestures of his hands. He had returned, it was understood, from a rather hazy career as professor of history in America to "tumble into a commission" and get out to France in the early stages of the war. To be a professor of European history and to assimilate whole-heartedly the statements of the official propagandists upon the causes and nature of the war requires a degree of mental elasticity that Dick Leverett neither possessed nor had any ambition to acquire. It seemed better, as things were, to stick to his views and enjoy himself; there were always one or two who from lack of anything better to do would listen, and Dick Leverett was happy enough when talking. This baby-faced individual in the next bed to him was just the sort of partner that he liked to have for his conversations—green, but not too green; a fellow who would smile in a sour manner when you tried him out with some remark about the privilege of shedding one's blood for the flag; a fellow who would attend keenly enough when you dropped some chance observations concerning the French policy of encirclement, or the financial relations between Poland and the Allied Powers, the courses of lectures delivered at Staff colleges since 1911 on the advantages of the attack through Belgium or the Vosges, the terms, as disclosed in America, upon which Italy entered the war, or the nature of the *Ruritania's* cargo. A good chap, Freddy Mann; a fellow to talk to; not one of these ardent unfledged public school patriots, or these "damn-you-for-a-Hun" Regulars, or these brainless long-suffering middle-aged business men who seemed to be pleased enough to do their bit. Incidentally, it was an advantage that Freddy Mann was near: Dick Leverett did not care to make himself conspicuous by walking about the ward; he preferred to do his work in corners, unobserved. He liked to borrow money, too, for drinks, and Freddy Mann's pockets were easily opened: he knew a trick or two at bridge, and Freddy Mann never objected to making a fourth at a quiet rubber, or meeting his I.O.U.s at the end of the evening. A good chap; he was sorry he was going; he wished he had come across him before: however, there was still a morning left, and the ways of Millfield suited Dick Leverett very well.

·   ·   ·   ·   ·

"But how do you know all this?"

It was not the first time that Freddy Mann, sitting fully dressed on his bed at 10.30 on a summer morning, had asked the question.

"My job to know. By the way, about that five bob I borrowed yesterday. I'm awfully sorry, but——"

"Oh, that's all right. Damn that. Then do you really mean"—Freddy Mann looked rather intently at Dick Leverett—"that it's all rot—all we're fighting for?"

"Well—hardly put it that way in public, perhaps, but—say it evens out, our side and theirs. War of defence—guard hearth and home inviolate—protect the weak—all that; you know—same for both, that's all I mean."

"Then the Boche and us——?"

"Two dogs fighting in the street, that's all. You don't believe it?" with a sideways glance and smile.

"I—I've wondered sometimes, you know. I remember once when I found a letter upon a dead Boche up at Hooge—a schoolmaster chap, written by his pupils—school somewhere in a little village in Bavaria. I remember I wondered then."

"I could have told you if I'd been there."

"And all this damned trench warfare—it's all just waste of time?"

"Well—good for the Regulars upon the Staff, of course, and the profiteers and people, but as for us——" Dick Leverett shrugged his shoulders.

"Way of enjoying oneself, I suppose. Some fellows batten on it. Can't say it ever appealed much to me."

"Yes." Freddy Mann paused. "You know, Leverett, that's just what puzzles me about you. You knew all this before. Why did you ever cross to join in. You needn't have done: it wasn't quite like us."

Dick Leverett in his turn looked keenly at Freddy Mann. Yes, he was straight, this fellow. And he wouldn't in any case see him after tomorrow. And he seemed to want an answer. What did it matter whether he knew or no?

"Got another five bob on you?"

"Let's see—don't think so. No."

"Glad of that. Because otherwise I'd have drunk it before the day was out. That's why."

A smile came over the loose flabby lips. Freddy Mann noticed, not for the first time, how bloodshot were his eyes.

"Follow?"

"No."

"Well, then—because it seemed the only thing to do. You see—it isn't as if I'd got a job."

"But, damn it, you're a professor."

"Was—Harvard, Yale and Lord knows where else. I repeat it, *was*. Still don't follow?"

"No."

"D.K.O., old boy—because of this, the drink, and—other things. They found out. That's why I thought I'd better come. Wife left me, you know—don't blame her—took the kids. Easy enough to do it there. Tried again, but in our job once you're done you're done. Tried scribbling, and odd jobs—then the war came, and so I came across to fight— for—the—dear—old flag."

"But if you don't believe any of this—what people say in England—why aren't you a conscientious objector?"

"Not me—no damned fear, not me. Bit of pluck that wants. Not in my line. Besides, had an idea I might make good, you know. Not that I have; they've caught me at it, tight on parade, playing the dirty at poker and things. No, Second Lieutenant Leverett hasn't brought it off. Bullet through the guts, and this." He looked round the bare polished friendless ward. "So now——"

"But can't you get out and make good again?"

"Not in me, old son. Tried it once, and all for nothing. Stay here now, if I can, till it's over, then slip away. Amuses me, now, to see those other warriors and fire-eaters, but it's not for me. As for being a conchy—why—they don't even have drinks at Dartmoor: so long as I get out a little every now and then——"

The hatchet-like face with its unsteady eyes and loose mouth turned again to Freddy Mann.

"See? Doesn't matter as far as I'm concerned. All a game. But just sometimes—when I see a chap like you— you're damned young, you know, and a damned good chap. It's the truth I'm telling you, God's truth, and they don't know here, or won't tell, and it's chaps like you that have to pay."

His voice sounded clearer and steadier than Freddy Mann had ever known it to be before.

"Some day other fellows will tell you—good chaps, not rotters that scrounge for drinks. But whether it's they or I that tell you, it's the truth. Got you, this merry-go-round that Europe's started—won't even let you get out of here to get a breath of fresh air on a summer morning. Got you. Thank God, it lets a man out sometimes. Gives you a chance to get a drink. No, it hasn't come off with Dick Leverett. Hardly ever does, though, if you act a lie. That's what I was doing, when I got a bullet through my guts."

CHAPTER XXVI

LIEUTENANT-COLONEL James Wingate, Commanding Officer of the Southshires Depôt, Carchester, was fortunate in that at a time when there was much unsettlement and looseness of thought abroad his beliefs were fixed and steady. Colonel Wingate believed implicitly and with almost equal fervour in the four cardinal objects of his faith—God, his country's cause, his regiment and the British soldier. He believed in God for the simple reason that it had never occurred to him to do anything else. The God to whom he had been taught to pray had brought blessings innumerable to the British arms: without Him, neither now nor at any previous time could anything that he or his countrymen had sought to do prevail. Some, he knew, spurned such faith or, as they called it, such superstition as this. But he knew well enough what it was that had supported the great soldiers of the past, and he was content to follow where Wolseley, Roberts, and Gordon of Khartoum had led. Nor, if belief in their country's cause was good enough for such men as these, did he see why it should not be good enough for him. And, however great his devotion to his country had been in the past, in the Soudan, in India or South Africa, it had never been so passionate as now. Was there ever a war in which the British flag had stood more visibly for the cause of righteousness. Martyred Belgium, tortured France—was ever the issue of good and evil more clearly manifest?

So much for the faith of every man, but Colonel Wingate swore allegiance in addition to the soldier's creed. Might Heaven but grant that the Southshires, whose history, as blazoned on banners stored in regimental messes or hung in cathedrals, had been so glorious, not be wanting now, when the greatest of all calls was made upon them. His responsibilities in this respect were heavy, for it was his duty to take those inexperienced and untrained civilians who poured into his depôt and imbue them within a few short weeks with that blind devotion to their regiment and reverence for its tradition which went so far to make the British soldier. Thank God that those with whom he had to deal were Englishmen: that granted, the rest would follow. The Englishman and the British soldier, in him in the last resort Colonel Wingate was content to pin his faith. How well he knew the British soldier! Hard swearing, perhaps, and hard living at times, but true as steel and unshakeable as rock in hours of stress—what heed did the British soldier pay to life or safety when King and country called him? Was there any limit to his heroism, to his blind obedience to the call of duty? All honour to the British soldier, and praise be that some at least of the grand old breed had survived those first few awful weeks, which might easily have spelt annihilation. So long as he had some to help him, and infuse their spirit into others—so long as there were still left men like Sergeant-Major Sugger, who, in a hurricane of shell-fire, had stuck to his post at Hooge till he became unconscious. With men like that by his side, and his God and country to sustain him—yes, the Colonel recognised it with thankfulness, he was fortunate indeed in that he possessed the soldier's four-fold faith. Would that he could impart it to others even more widely than he had. It was of that, more than any training or experience that those with whom he had to deal stood in need—those boys especially, those young rankers and subalterns, they needed it most of all. This young officer, for example, this Lieutenant Munn, or Mann, or whatever he called himself, whom Gregory, his second-in-command, had complained about—probably that was all he needed. Possibly Gregory was right in making a disciplinary matter of it—nobody could be allowed to misbehave, or sit grinning openly through a lecture on "The Soul of the War" by a visiting General, but from what he'd seen of him he didn't seem to be a bad chap; he'd seen some service, and he'd got a nasty wound. Probably that nine months hanging about in hospitals and in convalescent homes had soured him a bit—now that he was here, and getting down to the war again, it would probably be all right. Why not send for him, and have a chat? It was rather important, after all, that the officers who had seen active service should set a good example to the others. He'd have a chat. Gregory wouldn't know, and he didn't suppose he'd mind if he did. He'd just get him tomorrow evening, and have it out: help him to see things as they were, and give him a touch perhaps of the soldier's faith.

•   •   •   •   •

It wasn't quite so easy after all. Colonel Wingate was very glad that he had sent for the erring subaltern. Gregory had a habit of boxing up little affairs like this: he didn't really understand non-Regulars, who had been pitchforked straight from school into the war. He was always making mountains out of mole-hills: he probably would have done so this time if he himself hadn't stepped in in time. There was nothing after all against this fellow: he knew his job, and had carried out his routine depôt duties well enough. But it was a bit tricky. He liked the chap, but it was difficult to get at what was in his mind: and those rather hard lines round his mouth were in unpleasant contrast with his fresh face and frank eyes. He had apologised handsomely enough for that business Gregory had made all the fuss about: but it was more than that he wanted. Well, damn it, he'd gone some way in asking him to have a private talk at all: he wasn't going to be beaten.

"Well now, look here—I say, sit down"—in tones of genial imitability. "Never mind all that. We aren't on parade now. Look here." He prodded his writing pad with his pencil. "What would you do if somebody attacked your sister?"

Good Lord, the attack on the sister again. In spite of the unfortunate events of the preceding day Freddy Mann felt tempted to laugh aloud. It was always his sister. They started with that in 1914.

"Well——" He stopped.

"Go on."

"They haven't."

"Don't be a fool." Colonel Wingate had sat on committees dealing with conscientious objectors, and this gambit rarely failed to work.

"They've done the same thing. They fell on Belgium."

"Belgium! Why——"

But again Freddy Mann stopped. Why argue? He wasn't Dick Leverett. He stopped.

"There you are," the Colonel had scored his first point. "Worth fighting for them, isn't it? Your sister's honour is worth fighting for? Or perhaps there's a young woman you're interested in: no offence, you know." The Colonel spoke in a kindly voice, and he was a kind man. There was no suggestion of offence.

"Perhaps."

"Well, her honour. Isn't it worth defending?"

Freddy Mann had a shrewd suspicion that in any case his pretty little Irene's honour would look after itself in its own way, whether British or German were abroad: this also it was difficult to say.

"That's it—see what I mean? That's all it is, this war. That's what the British are defending, as they've always done—the weak and helpless."

Freddy Mann looked at the Colonel, his marks of rank, the ribbons on his breast. For thirty years he'd been defending the weak and helpless: roughly, he'd drawn in pay and allowances £20,000 for defending the weak and helpless. He'd earned the K.C.B., the D.S.O. and Lord knows what else for defending the weak and helpless.

He'd—he'd made a damned good thing out of defending the weak and helpless. He was a good chap, but it had paid him well.

"Don't you see, my boy?" The Colonel rose and put his hand on Freddy Mann's shoulder. (He would, thought Freddy Mann.) "That's all it is: you're tired, that's all—natural enough after Ypres and a nasty shaking-up like that. But just see it as it is. Think of the cause, and the regiment—that's something worth fighting for, too, the regiment."

More to fight for. There was always something new to fight for. There was humanity to fight for, Belgium, England, home and beauty, the putting an end to war, the liberation of Europe, and now the regiment. One tended to get confused. As for the cause of the regiment, he couldn't say that it appealed to him particularly. His own old crowd was one thing, but the regiment another. The Regulars had never seemed particularly anxious to see him. "Got to have these fellows in the mess, I suppose," they had remarked when the battalion had first arrived at Aldershot. "Oh well, it's only for the war."

"Damned hard on the Tightshirts to have these fellows round." Yes, the regiment. . . .

"Men like Sergeant-Major Sugger, you know. He's only one N.C.O. I know. But think of him, and all it has meant to him."

Yes, Freddy Mann was perfectly prepared to think of all it had meant to Sergeant-Major Sugger, but he preferred once again to do this in silence.

"And he's not the only one."

Freddy Mann was hardly surprised to know that he was not the only one.

"Think how many times those splendid fellows have stared death in the face."

Yes, when they couldn't bring off a Blighty.

"It's just the regiment, you know, the Cause, and—there's one thing more," in rather deeper accents. "There's God above, you know."

Was there then a God above?

" 'There is none that fighteth for us, but only thou, O Lord'—we mustn't forget, my boy."

"Gott mit uns." Freddy Mann thought of the metal clasp upon the belt of the first dead German he had buried, in those early days—that little schoolmaster chap with the letter in his pocket.

"And you still say you don't believe?"

It wasn't fair. Suddenly Freddy Mann's indifference changed to something approaching what he had felt on that night when poor Bill had cracked at Ypres. This was altogether so damned like an interview in the Headmaster's study two years ago; he was past this now.

"I'm sorry, sir—I haven't——"

"Never mind that, my boy; never mind. Nothing, that. Just a touch of the shell-shock. Never mind."

"No, it's not that. But—may I go, sir? I'll carry on as long as I'm here."

"Of course you will, of course, of course. Good lad. Get on with that bombing of yours. That's the stuff. Put some life into it. Tell the men about it, you know. Tell 'em about Messines and—the Cause, you know. We've got good enough bombs now. Kill anything within thirty yards. But that isn't enough—bombs aren't enough alone. It's the belief behind that's wanted. Just try to believe, my boy—believe—believe—let your sword be a sword of faith."

"I——" Freddy Mann stopped. Again, why argue? He only knew that British and Germans fought in the same manner, lived in the same manner, bled equally when wounded, stank and rotted the same in death. And this, after all, seemed about all that it was worth while to know. Perhaps the spirit of one was of God, and one the Devil. Perhaps the British soldier's life was hallowed in sacrifice, his regiment a holy thing. Perhaps, perhaps not, why argue?

"I'll carry on, sir, and do the bombing. It doesn't matter, as far as the bombing is concerned, whether I believe or not."

"But, my boy——"

"You can't believe without thinking, and I don't want to have to think. It was thinking that made me go mad that night. I don't want to go mad like that again."

"How old are you?"

"Twenty."

"Is there nothing you believe in?"

"No."

CHAPTER XXVII

"Now, mark you, lads, what you want to remember is that there's only one good German, and that's a dead 'un. Remember that."

Freddy Mann, standing by himself at the end of the field, watched with interest the red-faced Sergeant-Major Sugger putting the latest class of recruits through the first stage of bayonet instruction. He had during the last few weeks grown more or less accustomed to Sergeant-Major Sugger, more accustomed, perhaps, than Sergeant-Major Sugger had to him. It had at first been something of a shock to see the braggart so thoroughly established in a post of honour at the depôt, and Freddy Mann's first instinct had been to make some short but sufficiently clear statement on his military record to the Carchester authorities. But nothing, after all, was to be gained by that. Sergeant-Major Sugger was what he was, and in his heart of hearts Freddy Mann, his own ideals now dead, rather admired the manner in which he had "got away with it." That lucky piece of shrapnel that had got him as Harry had appeared round the traverse had just saved the situation: he had been carried down the Menin Road that night in the state of helplessness that he had striven to attain, and Carchester, as he had shrewd reason to suspect that it would, had taken him at his own valuation. There were few Private Bamfords about, few who were his equals at the game, and those few whom he had found were soon to their mutual advantage in league with him. Get the Regular N.C.O. to the regimental depôt, and his path is easy.

Sergeant-Major Sugger soon established himself on parade ground and in the sergeants' mess, and proposed now and for the duration to remain there and pass on to the youth of the country something of his spirit of martial valour. After all, why worry? If it were not him, it would be somebody else probably of his sort who would stand there twirling his moustache, every now and then seizing a rifle and bayonet and making some showy lunge at a red patch on a swinging sandbag, and mouthing like a gramophone the doctrines and exhortations that enable a man the more efficiently to strike steel through bone and flesh. Good old Sugger. That was exactly what Robbie had always said he would be doing in the second summer of the war. That's how they had pictured him, talking just like that.

"That's where you want to get 'em, me lads —there by the patch. Ain't no use ticklin' 'em, or takin' a bit o' cheek. Good and proper in the middle, then get yer foot on the carcase—carcase, mind—and get it out clean, with a jerk like this."

Out came the steel from the sacking.

"Red up to the 'ilt, that's what yer want to see. Inch or two o' red ink, that ain't no good. Red up to the 'ilt, and there's one bloody Boche the less—same as what we used to do."

He was, after all, so much of the spirit of the place. From Colonel downwards, they all taught this, and, it was to be presumed, believed in what they taught. Had he himself taught differently as he trained his bombing squad?

"And, mark you, the sooner it's done the sooner it's over, and you'll all be back at 'ome again. Kill 'em off and get it over quick."

The sun suddenly shone out and threw the scarlet patches that marked heart and lungs upon the sandbags into sharper relief.

"Get 'em there, and there, like this."

Sergeant-Major Sugger lunged again, driving his bayonet through the dummy's heart. The sand poured out.

"Imagine that's his guts. Only a swine's guts, after all."

Was he worse than others?

"That's yer job, me lads, to kill 'em off. That's the first job of any Britisher today."

The General had said the same thing in his lecture to the officers of the depôt the week before. Freddy Mann watched the group, standing attentive, rifles in hands, in the peace of the summer afternoon, and smiled. Was Sugger the only humbug and hypocrite? Weren't they all the same?

"That's how we treated 'em when I was there. That's how we stopped 'em up at Ypres—I tell you, lads, at Ypres. . . ."

But at that Freddy Mann came forward. He was, after all, in charge of the parade. He came quickly forward, and spoke to Sergeant-Major Sugger in a low tense tone that others could not hear.

"You can leave Ypres out of it. Don't taint Ypres with those lies of yours, or . . ."

"What d'you mean, sir?" Sergeant-Major Sugger stepped back.

"Leave Ypres alone, I tell you. You know the reason. Tell them any other lies you like, but you'd better leave Ypres alone."

CHAPTER XXVIII

H E was rather sorry that he had to take this road. He had no particular objection on other grounds to marching through the countryside of France at the head of a hundred ill-assorted N.C.O.s and men, some raw recruits, some grizzling and gloomy Regulars, some cowed or semi-mutinous conscripts. They had given him an efficient enough sergeant-major in Sergeant-Major Masters, when they had entrained him and his staff at Boulogne and told him to get them along to Bavinchove, and go to Watten. Sergeant-Major Masters was marching along in a determined manner at the rear, keeping them well together and taking no chances with the man lurching along without rifle under close arrest in front of him. He'd got them along without much trouble; not that, with Sergeant-Major Masters and his own experience, trouble would have mattered much to him. When that Irishman played up at Abbeville it hadn't taken more than a minute to get him fixed, and he didn't think that anybody else would try it on.

Drafts usually moved about France in these days in some such way as this. They were sorted out at "The Bull Ring," clapped into steel helmets, hung round with respirators and equipment and sent packing by a business-like major to their destinations. They were bundled from R.T.O. to R.T.O., fed by reluctant quartermaster-sergeants on the way, and billeted in a countryside that went about its work and regarded them with complete indifference except as a source of a few extra francs in return for the outbuildings that they hired. The taking of the draft was nothing, but Freddy Mann wished that his way had lain along another road. It was on just such a day as this that they had marched two years ago through the Forêt d'Eperlecques to Watten; and it was to Watten that they were marching now. The forest, as then, was green and peaceful; kids were playing in the little street of Ganspette as they were playing on that day when he and Robbie had strolled out after the day's march and given them chocolates as an aid to a halting conversation.

In Watten, too, it seemed most likely, everything would be the same. He knew before he saw her that Madame Fouquière would be sitting before her door, watching a battered straw hat in the little plot in front of her and noting with approval that its owner was bent well down upon his work. He guessed that she would regard their approach with a large impassive stare, following them with her eyes as they marched towards the estaminet. He knew the barn that they would occupy; the worst barn into which, being junior, he had had to put his platoon when they first arrived. He almost hoped that it would remain at this, that he might stay his night there, sleeping where he could and pass, still a stranger, to the east. But she called him as he stood with head averted upon the further side of the road.

"Come here, *mon Bébé*."

"How did you know that I am *Bébé*?"

"Sit down, where you used to sit. I knew."

Freddy Mann hesitated. The Sergeant-Major had gone on, and was entering the farmyard to the billet.

"He will arrange. Sit here. Are these your men?"

"Yes—no."

"And yours are there?" She pointed to the east.

Freddy Mann nodded.

"They are not alive now?"

"Just one or two."

Madame Fouquière continued her knitting, impassive and unmoved. "Sit as you used to sit. And you?"

"Oh I got knocked out last year: shoulder, you know. Lasted the devil of a time, but it's all right now. Just on my way back, you know."

"Back there. Yes, I know. And those men?"

"Just men I'm taking up. A draft."

Damn the *ennemies oreilles* and the warnings about spies. She was Madame Fouquière, and this was Watten. If she wished it he would sit and talk. But he wished he had not come. How the past was round them!

"Are they good soldiers?"

"Fair to average—not like ours. Wish I could have the old crowd here instead."

"That does not happen, when once they go that way. You did not know that when you went?"

"No."

"You know then, now. I wonder if this time you will return. Ypres may have to keep you."

"Yes. It's got a good many. It'll probably get me, too."

"And once you wanted so to go there. You knew so little, *mon bébé*. Let me see, you are older now. That girl?"

Freddy Mann shrugged his shoulders.

"Another?"

"Yes."

"A *marraine*?"

"Yes."

"*Bonne chance*. What you can take of life, that take. You are still young; you may not have much more. Your friend?"

"He is there. He is a captain now."

"He is not dead, then. Pierre is dead, and Rupert. *Que voulez-vous*? There are some that live. And France lives yet. Are you still glad to fight for France?"

Freddy Mann did not answer. Madame Fouquière would have known, if he had told a lie. He sat and watched the sun setting over the hills, and listened to the guns to the left. Oh God, the memories of this place! If only he could get away. Suddenly he threw away his cigarette and rose.

"Sorry, Madame. Afraid I must get along. I——"

"Stay here. You will go tomorrow. Sit quiet now and sleep tonight. Tomorrow you shall go to Ypres."

"Damn Ypres. Why is it always Ypres? You were right, you know, about that. It's always Ypres."

"For us, Verdun. For you—yes—it is always Ypres. Till God brings rest, it will be Ypres for you. Why curse, *mon bébé*? If you live, you live. If not, it is to Ypres that you will give your life."

"That's all very well, but——"

"Why curse?"

She sat still knitting, while the shadows lengthened and flashes began to appear in the eastern sky. Finally she rose.

"Come in and rest. Why curse? You will not choose. Life or death, it will be for Ypres, not you, to choose."

CHAPTER XXIX

YOU do not usually feel a peace steal over you if you move from the quiet countryside of France, through Steenvoorde, Abeele, Watou and on past Poperinghe to Ypres, particularly if every step of the way is dogged by ghosts that walk beside you and speak to you, first one and then another, of broken hopes and dreams that have ended in awakening. You will not as a common rule walk lightly, when you pass the gaunt asylum where the shiver passes down your spine, greeting the towers that loom before you as sign-posts to point you on the way you needs must go. You may glory in the unceasing roar of guns, that pour forth their tons of charged metal from hidden places where once three doled-out rounds a day were fired. You may, if you are made of the soldier's fibre, exult in thought of what is coming, but whatever else it be, it will not be peace that speaks to you as you pass on through Ypres, to the root of a tree whose topmost branches you used to see, with the dead sniper in them, on the skyline, to a lake the capture of which once stood as the end of all achievement, and on through the scattered bricks of Hooge. But to one of a thousand who have trod that way to join as the smallest drop in the waters the tide that is setting east to victory there may have come some knowledge that makes those other evils round, the insistent threat even, of that death with which a man is always juggling, seem of little import.

There may be little to live for, the smile that is half a sneer may be firmly set upon the lips, the long lines of those who toil up the hill and through the mud-drenched fields may appear but so many puppets drawn by invisible wires to a blind and senseless end, and you may laugh to think that the salvation of a few heaps of bricks, of what was once a city, could ever have appeared to you to be a thing worth while to achieve. There may be nothing else within your heart but some vague desire for a vengeance to be reaped before a bullet comes: yet, even so, you will walk your way more easily if you know that it is to your own that you return, that a friend of friends awaits you in some dust-strewn cellar, oozing dug-out or square of concrete in the middle of a wilderness of waste and ruin.

•　　•　　•　　•　　•

"I always thought you might come back to Wipers." Robbie spoke with that slow unemotional voice that Freddy Mann knew so well. "But it's damned funny, coming back to us."

"Damned good luck."

"Vicke may have had something to do with it. They say he tries to work it with his officers. Anyway, here you are. Maisey shoved you in "C" Company as soon as he knew. Jolly lucky, too, that we've still got Bamford for you."

"What's he been doing in the meantime?"

"Swinging it, doing damned good things in the trenches, getting promoted and broken, talking about South Africa and rum and you. And now he's where he was. So are we all, more or less—not quite."

"No."

Freddy Mann looked out of the door of the emplacement through the driving rain upon the hills to his right and an interminable expanse of mud upon either side of them.

"Shoved on a bit. Must have been odd, taking Bellewarde."

"It was: just walked along through it, then got stuck up here by Clapham Junction. Lost a good many, but we got as far as this."

"What's the game now?"

Freddy Mann helped himself to a whisky and tried to find a match sufficiently dry to light a cigarette.

"Inverness Copse and Glencorse Wood. Lord knows after that. We've got to take over from the Lancs up there tomorrow. They've had the hell of a dusting today."

"What's happening elsewhere?"

"Dunno."

"Nor I. They say they've got on to Langemarck, but——" Robbie stopped.

"Nobody knows anything, you know—we're just stuck here in the mud. Know where 'C' Company is, and that's about all I do know. Swimming somewhere, that's all we're doing. Still, I suppose it's all in the right direction. Ypres is further away, that's something."

"Yes."

"It's all right. It's still there. You needn't bother to go to look for it. Suppose you came that way today?"

"Yes—same old way, but I kept to the road at Hell Fire Corner. Rather jolly passing Hooge."

"Remember our do at Hooge two years ago?"

Remember—Freddy Mann looked at Robbie. Was he man or more that he had not changed? That night of the flare attack had seemed the end of things: and he'd had the Somme since then, and La Bassée, and Messines, and this. Since August 1st, this——

"Fattened us up for this show pretty carefully. But it hasn't gone too well. This filthy weather——"

"What do the men make of it?"

"What do they say they make of it in England?"

"Oh, victorious troops—always cheerful—advance singing to the attack—driving all before them—you know the sort of thing."

"So they still tell lies?"

"Wallow in 'em."

"Mm. Like to come and see?"

"Yes." Freddy Mann got up. He wanted to get out again. He had a platoon, as in the old days, men to work with, even if not those for whom he had learnt to care.

"Suppose there aren't many now that I know?"

"Damned few. Mitchell's here and Bartlett and good old Harris, but Bettson's gone, and Field, and——"

One by one, as Company Commander and subaltern wallowed along the line, Robbie poured out names of men, some remembered, others forgotten. No, few enough were left.

"The Somme got those who got away from Ypres last year. Would have got anybody, the Somme. Damned bad show, the Somme."

"Bad as this?"

"No, not as bad as this. Even the guns can't fire here—slip about in the mud. Mules and ration parties get drowned here if they leave the duck boards. There's a gun buried somewhere by Stirling Castle, and Lord knows how many Maltese carts and G.S. waggons. Nothing's ever been as bad as this. Here's your fellows. Come in. This way—back to the game again."

Freddy Mann walked along the line of shell-holes, each fringed by a few sodden sandbags. He greeted one by one the little groups of men leaning as best they could against the sloping sides, mackintosh sheets over their shoulders and sacking and bits of rag round their rifles. In the twilight and the drifting mist and rain it was difficult to find one's way. From time to time Freddy Mann stumbled over dead horses, half-buried bodies, strands of wire and water-logged stretches of empty trenches. The reek that he remembered so well lay over the hillside like a miasma, a concrete thing that filled his eyes and throat. The bursts of shelling and machine-gun fire passed unnoticed. Once a heavy shell plunged harmlessly into the soft earth a few yards from them, half burying Robbie and himself; once, as he moved towards the top of the ridge, he felt the wind of a sniper's bullet on his cheek; once he passed a group of stretcher bearers, sprawling over a few broken pieces of wood and canvas, head downwards in liquid mud. Before him, as he walked, loomed indistinctly the dark masses of Inverness Copse and Glencorse Wood, with the starlights rising between the outer trees and the jets of fire spouting from their foot, to mark where the front line lay; and here, a few yards from where he stood, a road, marked by torn poplar trees, ran downhill through the darkness, to Hooge and Ypres. "Back to the old game": yes, that was all that there was to it after all. They might be strangers, all but Robbie, with whom he had come to play it, but it was the old game that he was called to play, with the dancing lights around him in a circle, and behind him the shell of a city that had marked him for her own.

CHAPTER XXX

NOBODY would question the importance of the cause for which Freddy Mann strove. Nobody would deny that if you have to go over the top in the morning, rum is the one thing that the men must have, that the bread ration doesn't matter in comparison to rum, that the post doesn't matter, or new respirators, or pork and beans, or any damned thing in the world but rum. It is obvious that if by a twister of a Q.M.S. like Boles your platoon has been deprived of rum it isn't your fault if the whole damned show breaks down, that it's only rum that will get the men out of their shell-holes and on to Glencorse Wood, that they've got to be pretty well tight before they'll move a yard, and they can only get tight on rum: that therefore if the Q.M.S. has bagged the platoon's rum, then he'd better damned well get down to it and bag some more, seeing that there're only two hours to zero and the one thing the men have got to have is rum. Nor, on the whole, can serious exception be taken to Freddy Mann's manner of pleading: vigorous, perhaps, but not unduly vigorous: it's no use talking as if you were at a Sunday-school treat at Edenhurst when you're dealing with swine like Boles. If you don't stand out for your platoon, he'll do the dirty on you again: five days they've been here, lying in these shell-holes in front of the Wood, and they've done their whack as well as anybody else, and they've been crumped to glory pretty well all the time, and they're fed up to the teeth and you don't blame them. What's the use of smiling and looking pretty and nice about it when Boles has got the rum at headquarters all the time, lapping it up and then saying it's all been given out. If he hasn't got it then somebody else has—that knock-kneed puppy Briggs, probably, or Maisey and the Adjutant, or the Army Commander perhaps or——

"It's all right, Cherub, old chap."

Robbie spoke quietly, but his voice could be heard clearly enough above the roar of the field guns a mile away.

"It's all right: it's only a little mistake, that's all."

"Mistake be damned."

Freddy Mann half wept as he snapped and snarled.

"Damned funny, isn't it, that it's always a mistake where my platoon's concerned? Suppose it was a mistake last Friday when——"

"It's all all right. Just take it quietly. It's the same for all. It's——"

"Same for all, is it? Why, Briggs and his crowd over there are just swimming in it. They've got ours as well, I tell you; and if that's all that that swine Boles can say——"

"It's quite all right." Robbie came nearer, till his head almost touched Freddy Mann's.

"Steady, old chap, steady."

"What's the use of saying 'Steady'? Suppose I'm allowed to ask for rum, aren't I? Or perhaps we're all to be teetotalers, our crowd? Perhaps we've got to go over the top on water. Plenty of water about, anyway."

Freddy Mann laughed.

"Look here, Mann——"

"Anybody would think I was asking a bloody favour, from the way you all go on. It's 1 now, and we go over the top at 3, and just because my chaps want their rum——"

Robbie laid his hand on Freddy Mann's arm.

"You're with them, of course—I can see that. Just because you've got the blasted company——"

The grip tightened, but Freddy Mann took no notice.

"Orders are, rum was to be issued at midnight. It's 1 now, and what I want to know is, where's our rum?"

"It's all right, Mitchell—don't bother to wait."

Robbie looked over his shoulder.

"Look here, Cherub, drop this. They're beginning to notice."

"Oh, yes, pity that, great pity. It wouldn't do if they began to notice that I was trying to get their rum for them. Doesn't do, in polite society, to ask for rum. Sorry I've bothered you. Of course we'll be very glad to take water, since it's very good for us. Can't go wrong, if you stick to water. Come on, you——"

He turned roughly to Robbie.

"Go on, you're O.C. You get it. Boles has got it and I'm going to have it. Thought you could do it on me, between you—thought——"

"Cherub, you know what this means—if you go on like this——"

"Yes. Means that Boles has got out of his feather-bed, and that won't do"—in a high, mimicking, falsetto voice.

Robbie turned away.

"Damned well go myself and get it—that's what I'll do. Go to B.H.Q. and get it. Tell 'em there. That'll wake you up. Pity if Maisey knows. It's—hullo——"

"Got it, sir," as Mitchell gave the accompanying salute. "Corporal Barnes, he had it. Got it up there, and it just so 'appened that we came across 'im. 'E's a goner. 'Ere's the rum."

"Got the rum, anyway. Goner or not, doesn't matter long as we've got the rum. Let's get on with it. Come on, Harris, look after ourselves—we'll——"

He moved and found himself face to face with Robbie. "We'll——"

Suddenly his head danced a little, and his hands began to shake. He stumbled a step forward, and felt for Robbie's hand.

"I say, Robbie, I——"

"That's all right, Cherub—all right—that's over. Glad it turned up—all right——"

"Robbie."

"Have a drink—quickly. Drink this."

Freddy Mann stood still, trembling.

"Oh God, Robbie. It happened to Bill in a different way. I didn't mean——"

"I know. It gets us all at times. Go on, drink it up. I know. No, I wouldn't start praying aloud. Bad sign, that. Just drink it up and cut along. I'll be round before—before we go."

·   ·   ·   ·   ·

Anyway, he was praying pretty decently, that fellow in the shell-hole just to the left of him. There are all sorts of ways of calling upon God, ten minutes before an attack. Sergeant Sugger's way, for example—it seemed to have served Sergeant Sugger himself well enough, as a matter of fact, but it had never struck Freddy Mann as being particularly fitting or dignified. Then there was the whining, paling way, the sort of whipped-dog whimper; or the mixed assortment of oaths and blasphemies, mingled with confused appeals, which in the sight of the Almighty must surely leave the suppliant where he was. No, if one had to call on God at all, this on the whole was the way to do it. If God heard at all, he surely ought to listen when a man spoke steadily in a quiet voice, and just once told him about his little kid at home. "Oh God, oh God, help me"— yes, a very reasonable form of prayer. "Help me, help me," the words came to Freddy Mann as he stood and waited, while a luminous hand crawled round an invisible watch upon his wrist. It might have been better if he himself had spoken once, quietly, just like that, instead of doing what he had done two hours ago. But now he hardly needed to.

Rather hard on the war gods that were abroad that night, that they couldn't rob him of that peace that had fallen so strangely once again upon him. They'd told him on church parade that the spirit of God brought peace. They hadn't told him that an old lead-swinging soldier could do it by standing by his side and grunting; that shells could swirl overhead, and burst around him, and leave him as unmoved as if he were a disembodied spirit, watching the issues from afar; that the pressure of Robbie's hand, as he came up to him now at the last, when Fate would so soon reveal her secrets, would bring that final touch of strength to knees that an hour ago had been as water; that now, when after twenty heart-beats more he would rise, and perhaps walk forward, perhaps stumble headlong, he would look behind him quickly to a mass of broken buildings that he imagined he could see, and step with a quiet smile, whistle in hand, to the front of the shell-hole, facing eastward to the jagged line of fire.

"Oh God, give me strength."

"That's right, old chap. That's all you want."

"Help me."

"That's right. Come on now—come on, Bamford—we'll dodge your bullet—stout fellow—come on, all of you. Yes, it's all right, Robbie, we're all here, just behind. Come on, old chap—God's heard you—come along."

CHAPTER XXXI

BOMBS—BOMBS had done it at the time of Loos, or would have done it if he had had half a chance, and bombs would do it again. God—if only he had some of his old crowd with him now, or even some of the August crowd at Glencorse Wood. Rabbits or not, they were his battalion. As for the perishers in this company of his, the knock-kneed mob of conscripts whom he had to drive out of shell-holes and pill-boxes—if Wingate could only see them he wouldn't buck about the regiment quite so much. Be damned to the regiment, and the brigade and the whole division they'd jerked him into after that scratch at Herrenhage Château. He'd rather be with the old gang and his two pips than have a company of these undersized wasters. Still, there they were, and now he'd got them he'd make them get on with it. Time this mud-crawling came to an end, all this squirming and sneaking round pill-boxes, all this floundering up to your neck or being crumped to glory if you left the duckboards. Whatever sort of an end it was, it was time it came. Just over there was the place Harvey had been to, on the day he'd told him about when they were at Ypres. Gheluvelt—that was the place to get to: yes, by gad! and if he went alone he'd get there—out of this filth once and for all, and on the road to Menin.

Muttering, he knelt beside the sodden boxes and drew the Mills bombs out one by one, handling them almost lovingly. Nice little eggs, they were, to be sure—pretty little eggs. He'd just hang a few round him, like this and this and this—and use the first on any swine in his new crowd who wouldn't come on with him. Bombs, bombs, and get it over—damned muddle it had been, it was time to get it over. They ought to have got Ypres free by now—got to Bruges, Passchaendale, God knows where. He'd do it for them—nobody else seemed able to do it, but he would. Robbie would have done it long ago, or the Skipper or Bill or Harry—but they weren't here now. Only at night they'd come and talk to him sometimes, but he was alone by day. Bamford would have done it, too, but Bamford wasn't there either: there was only him to do it. Everybody else was stuck in the mud but him. Thought they'd done him down, but they hadn't quite succeeded: they never would do him down, so long as he'd got his bombs. He'd got them, and he'd get there now. Yes, there it was. He clambered out of the pill-box and stood looking towards a sky just paling behind a line of jagged poplars to the east.

Gheluvelt—that was the place to get to. Never mind what it stood for, or what it was all about. Never mind all that. It didn't need Dick Leverett to stand mouthing out there, yapping at him from just over the edge of that shell-hole, to tell him that. He knew it didn't matter, as much as Dick Leverett knew it. If Dick Leverett didn't take his ugly face away, he'd chuck a bomb at that to start with, just as he would if Wingate didn't get out of his way instead of wagging his pincenez at him and trying to get into the pill-box to argue with him, or Madame Fouquière, sitting by that bit of wire and knitting and talking to him of Ypres. He'd chuck a bomb at all of them if they didn't get out of his way. He didn't want any talk about it, or what it was all about now. He'd finished with all that; all he knew was he was going to get there. That was the way, straight up, straight along—there was Gheluvelt behind those trees, and bombs would get him there—not talk, but bombs, bombs, bombs.

•   •   •   •   •

The German sniper watched in the shell-hole, with his finger on the trigger of his rifle. He was doomed, he knew, but this did not worry him, as everybody else at Ypres was doomed as well as he. Knowing this, he could afford to watch the situation calmly, as it developed before his eyes. The British were coming on on three sides now; he thought, as a matter of fact, that a few had got round him, as bullets were coming from his rear. Never mind them—he'd just watch those in front, and pick off those he wanted. They came waddling along, like so many water-logged and overladen clumsy wooden figures, falling about, some getting up again and others lying where they were. There were plenty to choose from for the final pick. He ran his eye deliberately down the line: yes, on the whole that was the fellow, that fellow in front with his hands moving in and out of his pockets in funny jerking movements, and a grin, or something more than a grin, upon his face. He kept on opening his mouth, and jumping a little whenever he threw a bomb. He was just about the right distance, too—just right for a nice neat shot. He was coming on, still with his mouth wide open and his eyes twice as big as usual: he seemed an overgrown baby, all mouth and eyes and jerking arms and legs. Yes, he was the chap. He'd get him through the head—he couldn't miss him. Two steps more, and the sniper smiled as he bent his finger. It was a pity that he fell dead as he pressed the trigger, as it spoilt his aim.

•   •   •   •   •

There is no reason, provided you can walk, to think of mud as something other than it is. It is an evil thing, but, like other evil things, it can be evaded or overcome by the wit of man. It will drown you if you leave the duck-boards, but keep to the spider track across the wastes and you will be safe. It will cling around your legs, seep over your thigh-boots, ooze through tunic and shirt and bind your muscles with its clammy chill, but you can stand against it, sweep it from you with your hands and arms as you struggle forward, keep breast and head erect and win your way, struggling step by step, to firmer ground. It will not clog your pistol if you wear your lanyard round your neck, nor foul your food if it is stored on the topmost shelf inside the dug-out. It stinks, but it helps thereby to overcome other reeks more vile. It will pin you to your shell-hole, but it will stretch before you as a protective bulwark to prevent your being overwhelmed by the sudden rush of the counter-attack. It is an evil, but not the only evil, nor perhaps the worst. If you have been among those who have pressed on from Clapham Junction, past Weldloek and Herrenhage Château towards Gheluvelt and Menin, you will have known other evil things in plenty.

You will have lain motionless through the day before grey concrete squares from which machine-gun bullets directed by invisible hands have spat forth in intermittent streams towards your lair. You will have cowered, as you have cowered so often before, beneath bombardments, your legs, arms and body so many masses of quivering tissues which have long forsworn your mastery, and your head a sounding board for a thousand hammers: aeroplanes will have swooped low over you, raining destruction as they roar their way along the lines of shell-holes; skulls will have grinned at you from the rank undergrowth or between the twisted branches of Glencorse Wood; human forms stained red will have grovelled to you moaning; corpses mingled with sandbags will have formed your barricades; green sickly clouds will have drifted upon you, while you panted, your teeth tight set upon a rubber tube and your eyes peering blindly through great goggle glasses, smeared with dirt and moisture; shifting half-seen shapes will have come to gibber at you during your hours of fitful sleep.

It is when you can no longer stand that it is fearful, for then it ceases to be dead matter, and becomes, quite suddenly, monstrously alive. Then, perhaps, though not before, you may be permitted to resign to it the mastery, knowing that no human spirit can struggle for ever against a spirit more than human, that is alive as well as evil. It is when you lie headlong in the fields in front of Gheluvelt at midnight, the final goal of your achievement almost before your eyes, but your body crippled and powerless to move, that the dead mass round you begins to stir and breathe. It will work its way over you, covering legs and thighs and waist and shoulders, sucking aloud in its grim rejoicing as it draws you further and further into the depths of its soft spongy being. As the star-lights rise before you, they will be reflected in the big saucer-like eyes that are now so nearly on a level with your own. A myriad fingers will entwine themselves in yours, and shapeless legs will hold yours in a grip that no wrestler in the world could ever break. Its smell will fill your nostrils, and its wet lips will rise to meet you and stop your mouth with the moisture of their kiss. It will live, and, living, cease to be your enemy and become your friend. You have lost so much, and you are so very tired. Those that were with you at Hooge and Bellewarde have left you. A hope that was dead and had begun to struggle to life again has died its second death: a city that you half hated, half cared for has forgotten you, for it has had many to care for it and hate it, and you are far away. Why grope further like an animal, or wander through the filth of daylight any more? There is a Being here that will hold you, and never let you go: its embrace is soft, and already as you sink within it the pain that made you breathe in spasms is lessened. You have had no respite, and here at last is rest. The face of day is hideous, and the sun but shines to breed a greater foulness. Here, in your hiding place, you will lie sleeping, for the Being that has found you and taken you to itself will keep you, and will see to it that you do not start at any sound or open your eyes again to the corruption overhead.

CHAPTER XXXII

MURIEL, it was sufficiently obvious, had forgiven him—free and full was the measure of the forgiveness. Could she, she rightly thought, do less. Perhaps she had judged him rather quickly; perhaps she had been young, and hardly understood. After all, he had not been much more than a boy himself, and one should not be too hard. She knew better now: one learns a good deal after a year or so in war-time in a London office. She was glad that he was to be out of that horrid hospital and at Edenhurst for Christmas; it would give her a chance to show him, to let him know. She hadn't seen so much of him as she would have liked to, as he seemed always to be in camps or hospital when she had been at home. Well, she'd make up for it. Poor boy, to think of the time he'd had; to think of his lying out there, only a few weeks ago, with a broken leg; to think. . . .

The thinking, it appeared, was to be a co-operative process. John Mann was fully determined for the time being to put all gloomy reflections upon the Government's attitude towards the struggles of a hard-working and honest tradesman far from him, and see to it that that boy of his they'd knocked about so should see what a Christmas dinner should be like. Even, Aunt Jane reflected, even if this world was a vale of iniquity and wickedness—and she was sure from all she heard and saw, much as she tried not to see and hear it, that it was hard to disagree with what the dear minister had said last Sunday week—well, even then there was no reason why one shouldn't make the best of it, come Christmas, and try to cheer the poor boy up a bit, seeing that it must all worry him as much as it worried her. To Cousin Helen, to whom a captain was obviously of greater intrinsic value than a lieutenant, it was sufficiently obvious that Christmas was the one time when all members of a family who were trying to do their bit should be together, and try to get out of their own little grooves by finding out a bit more about what each other knew, and there would be nothing like a long Christmas talk to get at the full story of the mess at Passchaendale, if Aunt Emma didn't butt in too much with her eternal Pharasaical preaching—which Aunt Emma most fully intended to do, for if one couldn't put the highest aspects of the struggle before her nephew's mind at such a time as this, what, she demanded very naturally, could be expected to happen to the poor dear boy's ideals? And her choice of that little book, *The White Souled Warrior*, was most suitable, and she would give it to him in plenty of time so that they could talk it all over quietly round the fire on Christmas Day.

Mr. Farrant, Muriel's father, who had, it was to be gathered, fallen into a Government contract or two in the building way, which rendered the falsification of his prophecies as to the early end of a war of attrition a matter of slightly less concern, took a more direct line in the matter and contented himself with remarking that he would supply the fizz, and how the hell did John Mann or anybody else think they were going to get going without a dozen bottles. While all his mother wanted was to see to it that there was no nonsense with the cook, to know that her boy was happy, to tell God that she was thankful, and to keep a watchful eye on Uncle Wal.

Whether this last precaution was as strictly necessary as was popularly believed, there can be little doubt that the problem presented by Uncle Wal was no less difficult in 1917 than it had been two years before. In some respects, indeed, it was distinctly aggravated: for the fact that Uncle Wal had come into a bit o' money increased his standing with the ne'er-do-well elements in the population of Edenhurst, and tended at times to make him slightly self-assertive even when in the company of his cousins and "in-laws." A further difficulty arose from the habit which Freddy Mann had formed of seeking, quite unconsciously, of course, his company to a greater extent than was perhaps desirable. Even now, at this Christmas feast, when sundry sniggered accompanied observations and uncalled-for lapses into a species of levity of questionable taste, should have warned all present that Uncle Wal had better be kept in his place till "it had worked off a bit," Freddy Mann, it was regretfully noted, saw fit to forsake the claims of Muriel and the port and cigars which were thrust upon him alternately by Mr. Farrant and his father, and bury himself in a secluded parlour behind the shop with Uncle Wal.

This must, however, be said in justice that Uncle Wal, with a humility that years of steady repression had engendered, was among the first to realise the unappropriateness of Freddy Mann's action.

"Damned nice of yer, me lad, but it ain't yer place, not to be sitting here with yer old uncle while there's others round. That gel, for example—that gel Muriel—pretty bit——"

"Damn Muriel."

"Pretty bit o' goods, though, all the same. Fair knockout tonight. Bit o' gold stuff in 'er 'air, too: gives class, that does—bit o' tone. Sweet on yer, too, she seems. If she'd been like that before, p'raps yer wouldn't——"

He stopped.

"You mean Irene?"

"Yes: no offence, lad——"

"Of course not. Good sort, Irene—used to be. Damned good sort. I remember my second leave and that time in hospital. Gave them fits at Millfield, did Irene. But—no, Uncle, old chap, Irene's not her rival. She's in America now, my pretty Irene—film comedienne, you know. Saw her off last year. Thought it would break my heart at the time, and all that. But no, it didn't break my heart."

Freddy Mann lit a cigarette indifferently.

"Your case, Uncle. Have one?"

"Thanks." Under cover of lighting a cigarette Uncle Wal watched his nephew narrowly.

"You know, lad, seems to me you've hardened a bit like. Natural, of course, along o' this war. But it's working on yer."

"Strange, isn't it?" Freddy Mann's voice was hard and toneless, and he lit his cigarette as he spoke with an expression of indifference.

"No, 'tain't strange: it's natural. But it's a pity; and all these 'ere clackin' 'ens——"

Good chap, Uncle Wal. Unconsciously, as so often before, Freddy Mann warmed towards him. He could have gone soldiering happily enough with Uncle Wal. Uncle Wal didn't go down in the accepted circle of Edenhurst: so much the worse for them. He wasn't giving much away so far as the rest of the Edenhurst crowd were concerned; but it wasn't quite the same with Uncle Wal.

" 'Tain't as if I haven't watched yer, lad: watched yer since the beginning. You was keen enough then, time yer first went out. Wore off a bit even then, though, time o' Loos, when that gel played up, and then again last year, and now——"

He looked at his nephew, leaning slightly forward, and then sat back.

" 'Tain't I want to worry yer—not like that crowd in there," as he jerked his finger towards the doorway. "But it's just—no kids o' me own, yer know—and if I could be a bit of help——"

Yes, let him hear. Why keep up the artificial reserve with Uncle Wal? He'd seen a good deal, he might as well know all.

"P'raps you're right, Uncle. It's just—that the bottom's dropped out somehow. Sometimes does with fellows, you know, after they've been out there. Not with all—not with chaps like Robbie. But we aren't all Robbies—and—it has with me."

He helped himself to a liberal whisky, leaned back and smoked for a few moments before continuing.

"Seems to have gone, you know, just bit by bit. Look at 1915, for example—we were going through in 1915— damned lot of going through at the end of it. Look at the Somme, Passchaendale—all that: three years, and now——"

Poor spirited, but you have to pick your Greathearts very carefully if it is from boys of nineteen that they are to come.

"And all that rot they talk about it—war for humanity, war to end war, war for God knows what. Go and look at a battlefield, and you'll soon cease to believe that quack. Leverett told me a thing or two about that, I remember— Dick Leverett, you know—but I guessed before."

"You ain't the only one."

"Funny way to free humanity, to drive conscripts into Wipers with pistols at their heads—done that in my time, you know."

Freddy Mann looked half doubtfully at Uncle Wal. Was he giving too much away? He was a civilian, after all.

"Go on, lad—Uncle Wal don't split."

"And it's such bloody hell, you know. Fools like Farrant don't know what they're talking about. But when you've had two years of it—just hell—only thing to do is, not to care. That's what you learn after a time—just not to care. Pretend to listen when fellows like Wingate preach, but the only thing to do is not to care."

He stopped a moment.

"Funny way you'd be in if you did. Look at our crowd, for example. Pretty well all gone now—just Robbie left and one or two. But most of 'em went at the flame attack on Loos, and Mitchell went at Glencorse Wood, and Bamford's done—suppose his bullet came, poor chap—and Chips and Bill——"

He got up suddenly.

"Be damned to it all. I'm through. Got to carry on, I suppose, but I'm through. That's all it comes to—ceased to care."

"Nothing then, now, you don't care for? Bad, that, in life, if there ain't nothing left."

"Nothing: how could——" Freddy Mann stopped and flushed and Uncle Wal looked quickly across the room.

"Sure? Dead sure? Ain't there nothing left to care for?"

"Nothing: except just——"

"Tell me, lad: just tell me."

"Ypres. That's all. That's all there is now—Wipers. But it's that that Leverett forgot. That's all. Funny thing is, though, it sometimes seems enough."

CHAPTER XXXIII

H E'D stay here a minute or two, for here of all places in Ypres was where he would choose to be—here, between the ramparts and St. Jacques Church, before the tunnel where they had halted on that first evening, when Baggallay and Field and Bill were still with them, and Ypres and the war were new. He had come, as he knew he would have to come, for Ypres had called him back. He was afraid at one time last year that she'd forgotten him, but no, she hadn't done that: she wanted something from him still, and that was why he had not been left to drown in the wastes before Gheluvelt or allowed with the passing of winter to linger in hospitals or camps at home. He had come direct, and with speed, for the call was swift. There was no need for a Madame Fouquière to point to the red glare to the south, beyond the Lille Gate, or bid him listen to the incessant thunders round. But he'd always known at heart that this would be so, that one day Ypres would call him back. Why else did she allow Robbie to get him back from Forward Cottage, or that stretcher bearer fellow to find him just as he was sinking headlong in the mud last year? She always knew exactly whom she wanted, and how she wanted them. Some she wanted dead, like Baggallay, but others, like himself, were to remain alive, so that they could come to be with her at her call.

She knew him, too: he guessed that that would be so as well. That wasn't the midnight wind whispering between the broken towers of the Cloth Hall, that was the voice of Ypres. It was hard to know what she was saying, but it was to him she spoke. She knew him, as well she might: there wasn't much he hadn't done for her, or given when she asked it. Perhaps she was asking for more yet; he couldn't make out what the voice was saying, perhaps it was that that it was telling him all the while. He couldn't find out here, but he'd know perhaps if he went through the gate and down the road. It wasn't so far this time; no footslogging, like last year, to Clapham Junction and Glencorse Wood— no further than just past the White Château and on to the railway crossing and the little shrine, for the circle of lights was very close to Ypres, and the towers and ramparts were near to watch you, to see that you stood your guard. That was why she wanted him, because her hour of greatest need had come. She'd stripped him of friends, strength and hope, and she called him again now to keep barred the gates that bound the Menin Road. She'd taken all he had, but what of that? She wanted him, and those, he knew, whom Ypres wants have to come. And he could still hear her speaking to him, as he passed eastwards down the road.

•　•　•　•　•

Colonel George Harvey bent over the motionless form of his young company commander. For two hours on end he'd watched him, trying from time to time to detect the faintest flicker of his pulse, or the smallest sign of colour in the bloodless cheeks. He was breathing still, but it didn't seem that now he could breathe much longer, even if the shelling stopped and they could get him down to the G.H.Q. trench and back along the Menin Road. He'd asked for this, of course; sooner or later it had to come. For the whole of those last mad weeks, as the British line fell further back to the south of Zillebeke and the iron grip closed more tightly upon them here at Ypres, it seemed that he'd sought this end. What fury of possession was it that had caused him blindly to leave trench or shell-hole upon the smallest hint of attack or raid? What madness had been working which had led him so often to turn backwards and speak aloud to Ypres as if in savage rejoicing in the moments of most awful and paralyzing thunder? Partly, perhaps, he was himself responsible. Long ago—he'd forgotten, until Freddy Mann had reminded him, of that chance meeting before Witteport when he, George Harvey, had watched him bury those early dead, those first guardians of the Salient. It was he who had told him that June evening how they'd fallen hanging on. Perhaps it was just that—some madness of association and memory working in a schoolboy's mind.

But Freddy Mann was no longer a schoolboy, no longer the Cherub now. Old—old. George Harvey looked at those lines graven so deep in the white chalky face—the drawn lips and hunted eyes now nearly closed. His head had once been a mop, he remembered, of lighted curls—there were only dank, lifeless strands now where the gold had been. His cheeks had been full, his forehead white and clear—there was parchment now for skin, and cheek-bones showed high above the sunken hollows of his face. It could not only have been the schoolboy's madness, for Freddy Mann had seen too much. Perhaps it was just the old story, the old lust for death that would not come to end the torture when men sought it most. Or perhaps again not even that, but—George Harvey bent low as the lips moved to frame a trembling whisper. "We've kept—you—Ypres." Was it after all just that? Was Ypres to Freddy Mann, who had known for three years Ypres and Ypres alone, a sacred thing to be defended? Were the torn streets, towers and ramparts hallowed? He'd guarded Ypres, and the shattered spine was the price he had to pay. Was that, after all, the secret of the madness, that to him at least there had been a glory in the guardianship? Men had died, here and in olden times, for lesser things. Perhaps, after all, while still a schoolboy he had understood.

·　　·　　·　　·　　·

Hear, now, Freddy Mann, for the Voices are speaking clearly: lie still upon your stretcher, for you cannot move, and answer as they speak.

"You have returned: has all been taken from you?"

"All."

"Comrades?"

"Yes, comrades."

"And strength?"

"Strength also."

"And the hopes that once burned brightly?"

"They are dead."

"What have you left to dwell with you?"

"But memories."

"And to speak with?"

"Ghosts."

The Voices are louder. They are very clear.

"What do you seek now?"

"Rest."

"You did not know that this would be the end, the day you took the Road?"

"How could I know?"

"You had much to give. Were you ready to give it?"

"Yes, ready."

"And now that you have given all, and for you the fight is ended?"

"I am tired."

"Is pain yet with you?"

"I am past pain. I am tired."

"Is there anything you seek for?"

"Nothing, nothing. I am very tired."

"New life?"

"Not now."

"Or hope, or warmth, or friendship?"

"No, not now."

The Voices are louder: they are clearer yet. It is the Cathedral now that speaks, and the Church of St. Martin, the crucifix of St. Jacques, the Square, the Cloth Hall, the Menin Gate. And, as they speak, their Voices swell suddenly to a mighty flood of sound that fills the midnight, so that at last of their mingling is born the Voice of Ypres.

"Mine are high lessons, soldier: have you learned?"

"What lessons should a soldier learn?"

"Courage."

"I have learned much of Courage."

"Faith?"

"Yes, Faith—but I had forgotten."

"Friendship, too, so great that before it death is a little thing?"

"I have known such friendship: Robbie——"

"Sacrifice, also: have you learned to give?"

"I have given all."

"And Pain: is Pain your master?"

"No."

"Or utter Weariness?"

"I have fought Weariness and overcome."

"Death, then. Is death yet fearful?"

"I am prepared to die."

"These are high lessons: have you learned them all?"

"A little: I have tried——"

O mighty Voice of Ypres triumphant, speak!

"PASS ON, THRICE TRIED, TO
BE FOR EVER OF THE
BROTHERHOOD!"